The Little Big Book of Chills and Thrills

The Little Big Book of Chills and Thrills

Edited by
Lena Tabori &
Natasha Tabori Fried

Designed by
Timothy Shaner

A Welcome Book
New York

The publishers, editors, authors, and illustrator shall not be liable for any damage which may be caused or sustained as a result of conducting any of the activities in this book without specifically follow instructions, conducting the activities without proper adult supervision, or using proper caution. Extreme care should be taken with tricks, spells, and recipes involving the use of candles or fire.

Published in 2001 by Welcome Books,
An imprint of Welcome Enterprises, Inc.
588 Broadway, Suite 303
New York, NY 10012
(212) 343-0430 Fax (212) 343-9434
email: info@wepub.com
www.wepub.com

Designer: Timothy Shaner
Project Director: Natasha Tabori Fried
Production Editor: Alice Wong
Editorial Assistants: Lawrence Chesler, Serena Longyear

Distributed to the trade in the U.S. and Canada by
Andrews McMeel Distribution Services
Order Department and Customer Service (800) 826-4216
Orders Only Fax: (800) 437-8683

Library of Congress Control Number:
2001 132594

Printed in Singapore
First Edition
1 3 5 7 9 10 8 6 4 2

Contents

Stories

Poems

Spells

contents

Magic Tricks

Curses

Treats

Superstitions

Legends & Lore

Introduction

Ghost stories, superstitions, tricks of illusion, and things that go bump in the night. They're a delicious part of every childhood. But while our love and fascination with mystery and magic may begin when we are young, it can last a lifetime. Now in my mid-fifties, I am as much a Harry Potter addict as my 13-year-old godchild, awaiting the release of each new volume with giddy anticipation. I will never tire of the fantasy that there is a world beyond this one filled with fabulous beasts and mystical landscapes, where children can be wizards, dragons can be pets, and cars can fly through the sky like airplanes. It is in this spirit that we created The Little Big Book of Chills and Thrills. Nestled among these pages you'll find the best collection of scary stories, magic tricks, spells, superstitions, and legends we could find to enchant readers young and old (and aspiring wizards and witches!).

Real legends and curses, like those surrounding the creation of Stonehenge and the bloody hauntings of the Tower of London, are tucked between such terrifying classic tales as The Monkey's Paw and Midnight Express. For the practicing sorcerers, we've included some useful basic charms and spells. "Revenging Your Enemy," for instance, may come in handy in the schoolyard, while "Getting Rid of the Boogey Man" is a bedtime requirement. Fans of Houdini will devour the simple magic tricks like making a friend float in mid-air or an egg fly. You'll adore the bewitched recipes: Graveyard Brownies that magically melt in your mouth, Roasted Pumpkin Seeds that make the perfect Halloween snack, delicious Gingerbread Ghosts that fly off the plate, and many more. Finally, there are the stories behind common superstitions and even a few enchanted poems by such literary greats as Yeats, Shakespeare, and Kipling.

So turn down the lights, lock all the doors and prepare to be seriously spooked. This chunky little book will terrify, delight, and entertain you and your family for years to come.

A Moonlight Spell

Moonlight is the special ingredient of many spells and charms. For instance, reflecting moonlight off a mirror onto the face of a sleeping person will put that person under your spell. Moonlight can also be captured in water and used in a variety of magical recipes. Place a full jar of water outdoors beneath a full moon and let it soak up the moonbeams all night. Then recite aloud, "Moon spirits from up above, fill this jar with magic and love." Keep the jar tightly sealed until you need it to perform a spell or create a brew. One excellent mystical recipe that requires full moon water is Psychic Tea. Heat one cup of full moon water with 1/4 cup of mint leaves and a sprinkle of sugar. Simmer for fifteen minutes and strain. Drinking this tea before performing any psychic work will help focus the vision of your inner eye and heighten your senses.

THE CURSE OF
THE TOWER OF LONDON

The massive Tower of London is perhaps the most infamous and terrifying haunted dwelling in history. Built over a 200 year period that began in the early 11th century, this architectural wonder has 20 towers and occupies over 18 acres of land. Used by the English Monarch as a prison, the Tower of London has housed some of Britain's most notorious criminals. Murderers and traitors to the crown would find themselves hopelessly locked away in one of its many stone towers as they awaited their day of execution. Prisoners sentenced to death were beheaded within the Tower's formidable walls.

Many of those murdered on the block are said to haunt the Tower to this day. Lady Jane Grey, who held the throne for only nine days in 1554 before being executed in the Tower, is said to appear every year on the anniversary of her death, holding her head beneath her arm. Two other murdered

queens, Anne Boleyn and Katherine Howard, both wives of Henry VIII, also haunt the Tower as headless figures surrounded by a supernatural glow. Katherine has even been seen and heard wandering the halls begging for mercy as she did on the day of her execution.

One of the Tower's most gruesome murders was that of the Countess of Salisbury. As her head was placed on the block, the old woman panicked and tried to flee. The executioner chased her down and savagely hacked her to death with his bloody axe. It is said that spirits in the Tower still reenact her brutal killing for all to witness.

Of all the ghostly sightings in the Tower of London, the most disturbing is the apparition of two small boys walking along the hallways hand in hand. These children are widely believed to be the young sons of King Edward V. Edward's brother Richard, Duke of Gloucester, placed his young nephews in the Tower after King Edward's death. He later smothered the princes in their sleep, clearing the way for himself to assume the throne.

THE PHANTOM MESSAGE

Make words appear out of thin air in this trick that will give your audience goosebumps.

Before you perform the trick, prepare the magical note: Pour some lemon juice in a bowl and use it as "ink." Dip a toothpick into the juice and write on a piece of white paper. Keep the message spooky, such as:

I AM HERE. I CAN SEE YOU BUT YOU WILL NEVER SEE ME.

In front of your audience, announce that you are holding a message from the beyond. Push down the handle on your toaster, and hold the paper over the warm air above it.

The writing will magically appear.

The Song of Wandering Aengus

by William Butler Yeats

I went out to the hazel wood,
Because a fire was in my head,
And cut and peeled a hazel wand,
And hooked a berry to a thread,
And when white moths were on the wing,
And moth-like stars were flickering out,
I dropped the berry in a stream
And caught a little silver trout.

When I had laid it on the floor
I went to blow the fire a-flame,
But something rustled on the floor,

And someone called me by my name;
It had become a glimmering girl
With apple blossoms in her hair
Who called me by my name and ran
And faded through the brightening air.

Though I am old with wandering
Through hollow lands and hilly lands,
I will find out where she has gone,
And kiss her lips and take her hands;
And walk among long dappled grass,
And pluck till time and times are done,
The silver apples of the moon,
The golden apples of the sun.

MIDNIGHT EXPRESS

BY ALFRED NOYES

It was a battered old book, bound in red buckram. He found it, when he was twelve years old, on an upper shelf in his father's library; and, against all the rules, he took it to his bedroom to read by candlelight, when the rest of the rambling old Elizabethan house was flooded with darkness. That was how young Mortimer always thought of it. His own room was a little isolated cell, in which, with stolen candle ends, he could keep the surrounding darkness at bay, while everyone else had surrendered to sleep and allowed the outer night to come flooding in.

The battered old book had the strangest fascination for him, through he never quite grasped the thread of the story. It was called *The Midnight Express*, and there was one illustration, on the fiftieth page, at which he could never bear to look. It frightened him.

Young Mortimer never understood the effect of that picture on him. He was an imaginative, but not a neurotic youngster; and he avoided that fiftieth page as he might have hurried past a dark corner on the stairs when he was six years old, or as the grown man on the lonely road, in the *Ancient Mariner*, who, having once looked round, walks on, and turns no more his head. There was nothing in the picture—

apparently—to account for this haunting dread. Darkness, indeed, was almost its chief characteristic. It showed an empty railway platform—at night—lit by a single dreary lamp; an empty railway platform that suggested a deserted and lonely junction in some remote part of the country. There was only one figure on the platform: the dark figure of a man, standing almost directly under the lamp, with his face turned away toward the black mouth of a tunnel, which—for some strange reason—plunged the imagination of the child into a pit of horror. The man seemed to be listening. His attitude was tense, expectant, as though he were awaiting some fearful tragedy. There was nothing in the text, so far as the child read, and could understand, to account for this waking nightmare. He could neither resist the fascination of the book, nor face that picture in the stillness and loneliness of the night. He pinned it down to the page facing it, with two long pins, so that he should not come upon it by accident. Then he determined to read the whole story through. But, always, before he came to page fifty, he fell asleep; and the outlines of what he had read were blurred; and the next night he had to begin again; and again, before he came to the fiftieth page, he fell asleep.

He grew up, and forgot all about the book and the picture. But half way through his life, at that strange and critical time when Dante entered the dark wood, leaving the direct path behind him, he found himself, a little before midnight, waiting for a train at a lonely junction; and, as the station clock began to strike twelve, he remem-

bered; remembered like a man awaking from a long dream—

There, under the single dreary lamp, on the long glimmering platform, was the dark and solitary figure that he knew. Its face was turned away from him toward the black mouth of the tunnel. It seemed to be listening, tense, expectant, just as it had been thirty-eight years ago.

But he was not frightened now, as he had been in childhood. He would go up to that solitary figure, confront it, and see the face that had so long been hidden, so long averted from him. He would walk up quietly, and make some excuse for speaking to it: he would ask it, for instance, if the train was going to be late. It should be easy for a grown man to do this; but his hands were clenched, when he took the first step, as if he, too, were tense and expectant. Quietly, but with the old vague instincts awaking, he went toward the dark figure under the lamp, passed it, swung round abruptly to speak to it; and saw—without speaking, without being able to speak—

It was himself—staring back at himself—as in some mocking mirror, his own eyes alive in his own white face, looking into his own eyes, alive—

The nerves of his heart tingled as though their own electric currents would paralyze it. A wave of panic went through him. He turned, gasped, stumbled, broke into a blind run, out through the deserted and echoing ticket office, on to the long moonlit road behind the station. The whole countryside seemed to be utterly deserted. the moonbeams flooded it with the loneliness of their own deserted satellite.

He paused for a moment, and heard, like the echo of his own footsteps, the stumbling run of something that followed over the wooden floor within the ticket office. Then he abandoned himself shamelessly to his fear; and ran, sweating like a terrified beast, down the long white road between the two endless lines of ghostly poplars each answering another, into what seemed an infinite distance. On one side of the road there was a long straight canal, in which one of the lines of poplars was again endlessly reflected. He heard the footsteps echoing behind him. They seemed to be slowly, but steadily, gaining upon him. A quarter of a mile away, he saw a small white cottage by the roadside, a white cottage with two dark windows and a door that somehow suggested a human face. He thought to himself that, if he could reach it in time, he might find shelter and security—escape.

The thin implacable footsteps, echoing his own, were still some way off when he lurched, gasping, into the little porch; rattled the latch, thrust at the door, and found it locked against him. There was no bell or knocker. He pounded on the wood with his fists until his knuckles bled. The response was horribly slow. At last, he heard heavier footsteps within the cottage. Slowly they descended the creaking stair. Slowly the door was unlocked. A tall shadowy figure stood before him, holding a lighted candle, in such a way that he could see little either of the holder's face or form; but to his dumb horror there seemed to be a cerecloth wrapped round the face.

No words passed between them. The figure beckoned him in; and, as he obeyed, it locked the door behind him. Then, beckoning him again, without a word, the figure went before him up the crooked stair, with the ghostly candle casting huge and grotesque shadows on the whitewashed walls and ceiling.

They entered an upper room, in which there was a bright fire burning, with an armchair on either side of it, and a small oak table, on which there lay a battered old book, bound in dark red buckram. It seemed as though the guest had been long expected and all things were prepared.

The figure pointed to one of the armchairs, placed the candlestick on the table by the book (for there was no other light but that of the fire) and withdrew without a word, locking the door behind him.

Mortimer looked at the candlestick. It seemed familiar. The smell of the guttering wax brought back the little room in the old Elizabethan house. He picked up the book with trembling fingers. He recognized it at once, though he had long forgotten everything about the story. He remembered the ink stain on the title page; and then, with a shock of recollection, he came on the fiftieth page, which he had pinned down in childhood. The pins were still there. He touched them again—the very pins which his trembling childish fingers had used so long ago.

He turned back to the beginning. He was determined to read it to the end now, and discover what it all was about. He felt that it must

all be set down there, in print; and, though in childhood he could not understand it, he would be able to fathom it now.

It was called *The Midnight Express*; and, as he read the first paragraph, it began to dawn upon him slowly, fearfully, inevitably—

It was the story of a man who, in childhood, long ago, had chanced upon a book, in which there was a picture that frightened him. He had grown up and forgotten it, and one night, upon a lonely railway platform, he had found himself in the remembered scene of the picture; he had confronted the solitary figure under the lamp; recognized it, and fled in panic. He had taken shelter in a wayside cottage; had been led to an upper room, found the book awaiting him and had begun to read it right through, to the very end, at last.— And this book, too, was called The Midnight Express. *And it was the story of a man who, in childhood—It would go on thus, forever and forever, and forever. There was no escape.*

But when the story came to the wayside cottage, for the third time, a deeper suspicion began to dawn upon him, slowly, fearfully, inevitably— Although there was no escape, he could at least try to grasp more clearly the details of the strange circle, the fearful wheel, in which he was moving.

There was nothing new about the details. They had been there all the time; but he had not grasped their

significance. That was all. *The strange and dreadful being that had led him up the crooked stair—who and what was That?*

The story mentioned something that had escaped him. The strange host, who had given him shelter, was about his own height. Could it be that he also—And was this why the face was hidden?

At the very moment when he asked himself that question, he heard the click of the key in the locked door.

The strange host was entering—moving toward him from behind—casting a grotesque shadow, larger than human, on the white walls in the guttering candlelight.

It was there, seated on the other side of the fire, facing him. With a horrible nonchalance, as a woman might prepare to remove a veil, it raised its hands to unwind the cerecloth from its face. He knew to whom it would belong. But would it be dead or living?

There was no way out but one. As Mortimer plunged forward and seized the tormentor by the throat, his own throat was gripped with the same brutal force. The echoes of their strangled cry were indistinguishable; and when the last confused sounds died out together, the stillness of the room was so deep that you might have heard—the ticking of the old grandfather clock, and the long-drawn rhythmical "ah" of the sea, on a distant coast, thirty-eight years ago.

But Mortimer had escaped at last. Perhaps, after all, he had caught the midnight express.

It was a battered old book, bound in red buckram . . .

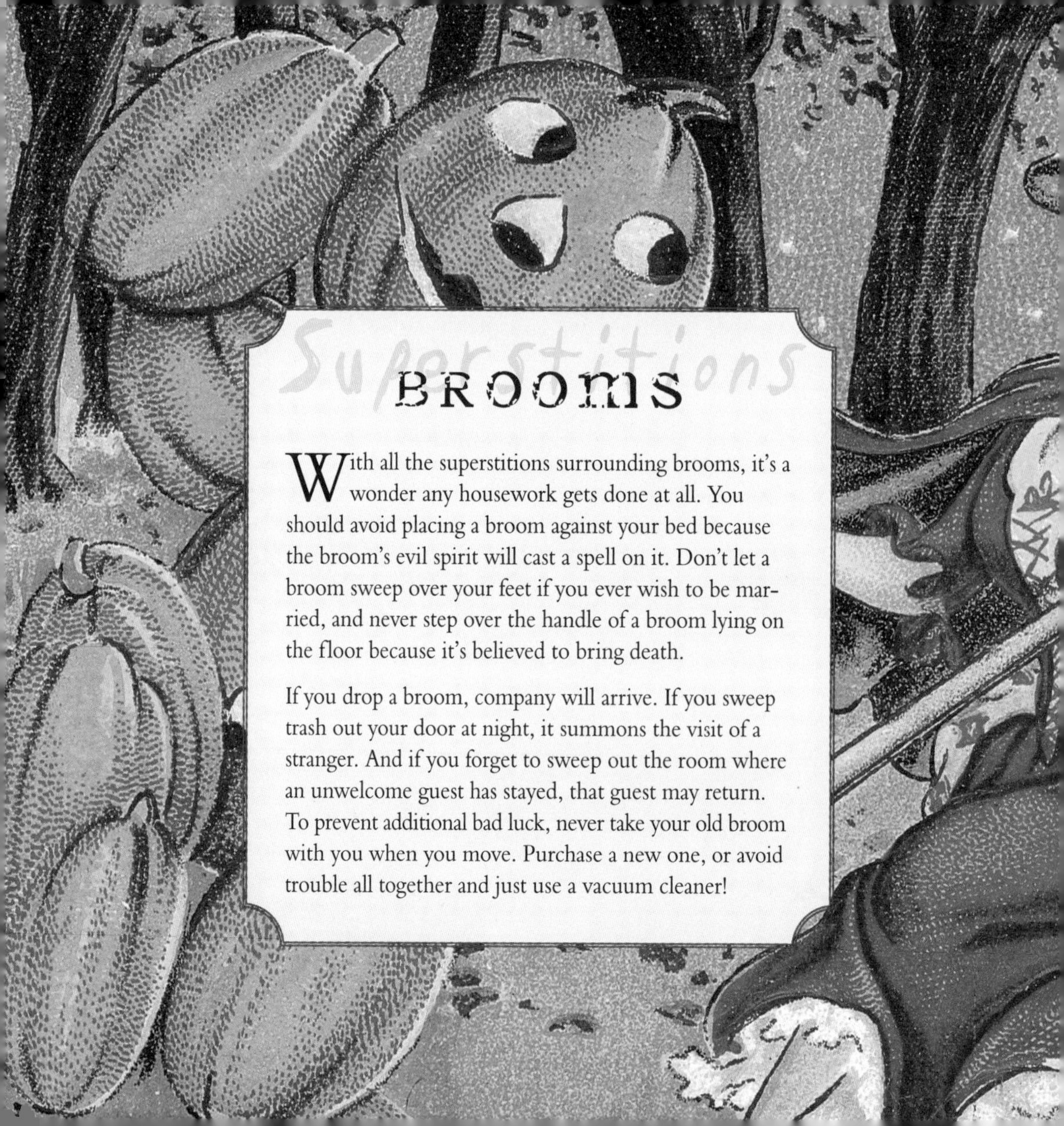

BROOMS

With all the superstitions surrounding brooms, it's a wonder any housework gets done at all. You should avoid placing a broom against your bed because the broom's evil spirit will cast a spell on it. Don't let a broom sweep over your feet if you ever wish to be married, and never step over the handle of a broom lying on the floor because it's believed to bring death.

If you drop a broom, company will arrive. If you sweep trash out your door at night, it summons the visit of a stranger. And if you forget to sweep out the room where an unwelcome guest has stayed, that guest may return. To prevent additional bad luck, never take your old broom with you when you move. Purchase a new one, or avoid trouble all together and just use a vacuum cleaner!

The Tempest

by William Shakespeare

These our actors,
As I foretold you, were all spirits and
Are melted into air, into thin air;
And, like the baseless fabric of this vision,
The cloud-capped towers, the gorgeous palaces,
The solemn temples, the great globe itself,
Yea, all which it inherit, shall dissolve,
And, like this insubstantial pageant faded,
Leave not a rack behind. We are such stuff
As dreams are made on, and our little life
Is rounded with a sleep.

Superstitions

Stonehenge

Built over four thousand years ago, Stonehenge, the massive stone monument that sits on the Salisbury Plains of England, is shrouded in mystery and legend. Was it constructed as an ancient calendar, used to predict astrological events or seasonal changes? Or was it a place of worship, a spiritual temple built to honor the deities of its makers? The purpose of this spectacular man-made rock formation has been studied and debated for centuries. Just as bewildering is the question of how Stonehenge was created. Some of the stones used are believed to have come from Wales on Britain's southern shores, hundreds of miles away. How these rocks, many weighing up to four tons, were transported such a distance in an ancient era before the invention of the wheel is a mystery. Many supernatural and mystical theories have been offered as explanation, though none have ever been proven. Some believe Stonehenge was the creation of alien life forms, while others claim that the great sorcerer Merlin used his magical powers to move the stones across land and sea. One legend even tells of the Devil creating Stonehenge as part of a bizarre riddle he concocted to toy with the local villagers.

Whatever the methods and intentions of it's builders, Stonehenge stands today as an awesome reminder that the world is full of unexplained mysteries and secrets.

The Hobbit

by JRR Tolkien

Deep down here by the dark water lived old Gollum, a small slimy creature. I don't know where he came from, nor who or what he was. He was Gollum—as dark as darkness, except for two big round pale eyes in his thin face. He had a little boat, and he rowed about quite quietly on the lake; for lake it was, wide and deep and deadly cold. He paddled it with large feet dangling over the side, but never a ripple did he make. Not he. He was looking out of his pale lamp-like eyes for blind fish, which he grabbed with his long fingers as quick as thinking. He liked meat too. Goblin he thought good, when he could get it; but he took care they never found him out. He just throttled them from behind, if they ever came down alone anywhere near the edge of the water, while he was prowling about. . . .

Actually Gollum lived on a slimy island of rock in the middle of the lake. He was watching Bilbo now from the distance with his pale eyes like telescopes. Bilbo could not see him, but he was wondering a lot about Bilbo, for he could see that he was no goblin at all.

Gollum got into his boat and shot off from the island, while Bilbo was sitting on the brink altogether flummoxed and at the end of his way and his wits. Suddenly up came Gollum and whispered and hissed:

"Bless us and splash us, my preciousssss! I guess it's a choice feast; at least a tasty morsel it'd make us, gollum!" And when he said *gollum* he made a horrible swallowing noise in his throat. That is how he got his name, though he always called himself 'my precious'.

The hobbit jumped nearly out of his skin when the hiss came in his ears, and he suddenly saw the pale eyes sticking out at him.

"Who are you?" he said, thrusting his dagger in front of him.

"What iss he, my preciouss?" whispered Gollum (who always spoke to himself through never having anyone else to speak to). This is what he had come to find out, for he was not really very hungry at the moment, only curious; otherwise he would have grabbed first and whispered afterwards.

"I am Mr. Bilbo Baggins. I have lost the dwarves and I have lost the wizard, and I don't know where I am; and I don't want to know, if only I can get away."

"What's he got in his handses?" said Gollum, looking at the sword, which he did not quite like.

"A sword, a blade which came out of Gondolin!"

"Sssss," said Gollum, and became quite polite. "Praps ye sits here and chats with it a bitsy, my preciousss. It like riddles, praps it does, does it?" He was anxious to appear friendly, at any rate for the moment, and until he found out more about the sword and the hobbit,

whether he was quite alone really, whether he was good to eat, and whether Gollum was really hungry. Riddles were all he could think of. Asking them, and sometimes guessing them, had been the only game he had ever played with other funny creatures sitting in their holes in the long, long ago, before he lost all his friends and was driven away, alone, and crept down, down, into the dark under the mountains.

"Very well," said Bilbo, who was anxious to agree, until he found out more about the creature, whether he was quite alone, whether he was fierce or hungry, and whether he was a friend of the goblins.

"You ask first," he said, because he had not had time to think of a riddle. So Gollum hissed:

What has roots as nobody sees,
Is taller than trees
Up, up it goes,
And yet never grows?

"Easy!" said Bilbo. "Mountain, I suppose."

"Does it guess easy? It must have a competition with us, my preciouss! If precious asks, and it doesn't answer, we eats it, my preciousss. If it asks us, and we doesn't answer, then we does what it wants, eh? We shows it the way out, yes!"

"All right!" said Bilbo, not daring to disagree, and nearly bursting

his brain to think of riddles that could save him from being eaten.

Thirty white horses on a red hill,
First they champ,
Then they stamp,
Then they stand still.

That was all he could think of to ask—the idea of eating was rather on his mind. It was rather an old one, too, and Gollum knew the answer as well as you do.

"Chestnuts, chestnuts," he hissed. "Teeth! teeth! my preciousss; but we has only six!" Then he asked his second:

Voiceless it cries,
Wingless flutters,
Toothless bites,
Mouthless mutters.

"Half a moment!" cried Bilbo, who was still thinking uncomfortably about eating. Fortunately he had once heard something rather like this before, and getting his wits back he thought of the answer. "Wind, wind of course," he said, and he was so pleased that he made up one on the spot. "This'll puzzle the nasty little underground creature," he thought:

An eye in a blue face
Saw an eye in a green face.
"That eye is like to this eye"
Said the first eye,
"But in low place
Not in high place."

"Ss, ss, ss," said Gollum. He had been underground a long long time, and was forgetting this sort of thing. But just as Bilbo was beginning to hope that the wretch would not be able to answer, Gollum brought up memories of ages and ages and ages before, when he lived with his grandmother in a hole in a bank by a river. "Sss, sss, my preciouss," he said. "Sun on the daisies it means, it does. . . ."

Then he thought the time had come to ask something hard and horrible. This is what he said:

This thing all things devours:
Birds, beasts, trees, flowers;
Gnaws iron, bites steel;
Grinds hard stones to meal;
Slays king, ruins town,
And beats high mountain down.

Poor Bilbo sat in the dark thinking of all the horrible names of all the

giants and ogres he had ever heard told of in tales, but not one of them had done all these things. He had a feeling that the answer was quite different and that he ought to know it, but he could not think of it. He began to get frightened, and that is bad for thinking. Gollum began to get out of his boat. He flapped into the water and paddled to the bank; Bilbo could see his eyes coming towards him. His tongue seemed to stick in his mouth; he wanted to shout out: "Give me more time! Give me time!" But all that came out with a sudden squeal was:

"Time! Time!"

Bilbo was saved by pure luck. For that of course was the answer.

Gollum was disappointed once more; and now he was getting angry, and also tired of the game. It had made him very hungry indeed. This time he did not go back to the boat. He sat down in the dark by Bilbo. That made the hobbit most dreadfully uncomfortable and scattered his wits.

"It's got to ask uss a quesstion, my preciouss, yes, yess, yesss. Jusst one more question to guess, yes, yess," said Gollum.

But Bilbo simply could not think of any question with that nasty wet cold thing sitting next to him, and pawing and poking him. He scratched himself, he pinched himself; still he could not think of anything.

"Ask us! ask us!" said Gollum.

Bilbo pinched himself and slapped himself; he gripped on his little sword; he even felt in his pocket with his other hand. There he found the ring he had picked up in the passage and forgotten about.

"What have I got in my pocket?" he said aloud. He was talking to himself, but Gollum thought it was a riddle, and he was frightfully upset.

"Not fair! not fair!" he hissed. "It isn't fair, my precious, is it, to ask us what it's got in its nassty little pocketses?"

Bilbo seeing what had happened and having nothing better to ask stuck to his question. "What have I got in my pocket?" he said louder.

"S-s-s-s-s," hissed Gollum. "It must give us three guesseses, my preciouss, three guesseses."

"Very well! Guess away!" said Bilbo.

"Handses!" said Gollum.

"Wrong," said Bilbo, who had luckily just taken his hand out again. "Guess again!"

"S-s-s-s-s," said Gollum more upset than ever. He thought of all the things he kept in his own pockets: fishbones, goblins' teeth, wet shells, a bit of bat-wing, a sharp stone to sharpen his fangs on, and other nasty things. He tried to think what other people kept in their pockets.

"Knife!" he said at last.

"Wrong!" said Bilbo, who had lost his some time ago. "Last guess! . . ."

"Come on!" said Bilbo. "I am waiting!" He tried to sound bold and cheerful, but he did not feel at all sure how the game was going to end, whether Gollum guessed right or not.

"Time's up!" he said.

"String, or nothing!" shrieked Gollum, which was not quite fair—working in two guesses at once.

"Both wrong," cried Bilbo very much relieved; and he jumped at once to his feet, put his back to the nearest wall, and held out his little sword. He knew, of course, that the riddle-game was sacred and of immense antiquity, and even wicked creatures were afraid to cheat when they played at it. But he felt he could not trust this slimy thing to keep any promise at a pinch. Any excuse would do for him to slide out of it. And after all that last question had not been a genuine riddle according to the ancient laws.

But at any rate Gollum did not at once attack him. He could see the sword in Bilbo's hand. He sat still, shivering and whispering. At last Bilbo could wait no longer.

"Well?" he said. "What about your promise? I want to go. You must show me the way."

"Did we say so, precious? Show the nassty little Baggins the way out, yes, yes. But what has it got in its pocketses, eh? Not string, precious, but not nothing. Oh no! gollum!"

"Never you mind," said Bilbo. "A promise is a promise."

"Cross it is, impatient, precious," hissed Gollum. "But it must wait, yes it must. We can't go up the tunnels so hasty. We must go and get some things first, yes, things to help us."

"Well, hurry up!" said Bilbo, relieved to think of Gollum going away. He thought he was just making an excuse and did not mean to come back. What was Gollum talking about? What useful thing could he keep out on the dark lake? But he was wrong. Gollum did mean to come back. He was angry now and hungry. And he was a miserable wicked creature, and already he had a plan.

Not far away was his island, of which Bilbo knew nothing, and there in his hiding-place he kept a few wretched oddments, and one very beautiful thing, very beautiful, very wonderful. He had a ring, a golden ring, a precious ring.

"My birthday-present!" he whispered to himself, as he had often done in the endless dark days. "That's what we wants now, yes; we wants it!"

He wanted it because it was a ring of power, and if you slipped that ring on your finger, you were invisible; only in the full sunlight could you be seen, and then only by your shadow, and that would be shaky and faint.

"My birthday-present! It came to me on my birthday, my precious." So he had always said to himself. But who knows how Gollum came by that present, ages ago in the old days when such rings were still

at large in the world? Perhaps even the Master who ruled them could not have said. Gollum used to wear it at first, till it tired him; and then he kept it in a pouch next his skin, till it galled him; and now usually he hid it in a hole in the rock on his island, and was always going back to look at it. And still sometimes he put it on, when he could not bear to be parted from it any longer, or when he was very, very, hungry, and tired of fish. Then he would creep along dark passages looking for stray goblins. He might even venture into places where the torches were lit and made his eyes blink and smart; for he would be safe. Oh yes, quite safe. No one would see him, no one would notice him, till he had his fingers on their throat. Only a few hours ago he had worn it, and caught a small goblin-imp. How it squeaked! He still had a bone or two left to gnaw, but he wanted something softer.

"Quite safe, yes," he whispered to himself. "It won't see us, will it my precious? No. It won't see us, and its nasty little sword will be useless, yes quite."

That is what was in his wicked little mind, as he slipped suddenly from Bilbo's side, and flapped back to his boat, and went off into the dark. Bilbo thought he had heard the last of him. Still he waited a while; for he had no idea how to find his way out alone.

Suddenly he heard a screech. It sent a shiver down his back. Gollum was cursing and wailing away in the gloom, not very far off by the sound of it. He was on his island, scrabbling here and there, search-

ing and seeking in vain.

"Where is it? Where is it?" Bilbo heard him crying. "Losst it is, my precious, lost, lost! Curse us and crush us, my precious is lost!"

"What's the matter?" Bilbo called. "What have you lost?"

"It mustn't ask us," shrieked Gollum. "Not its business, no, gollum! It's losst, gollum, gollum, gollum."

"Well, so am I," cried Bilbo, "and I want to get unlost. And I won the game, and you promised. So come along! Come and let me out, and then go on with your looking!" Utterly miserable as Gollum sounded, Bilbo could not find much pity in his heart, and he had a feeling that anything Gollum wanted so much could hardly be something good. "Come along!" he shouted.

"No, not yet, precious!" Gollum answered. "We must search for it, it's lost, gollum."

"But you never guessed my last question, and you promised," said Bilbo.

"Never guessed!" said Gollum. Then suddenly out of the gloom came a sharp hiss. "What has it got in its pocketses? Tell us that. It must tell first."

As far as Bilbo knew, there was no particular reason why he should not tell. Gollum's mind had jumped to a guess quicker than his; naturally, for Gollum had brooded for ages on this one thing, and he was always afraid of its being stolen. But Bilbo was annoyed at the delay. After all, he had won the game, pretty fairly, at a horrible risk.

"Answers were to be guessed not given," he said.

"But it wasn't a fair question," said Gollum. "Not a riddle, precious no."

"Oh well, if it's a matter of ordinary questions," Bilbo replied, "then I asked one first. What have you lost? Tell me that!"

"What has it got in its pocketses?" The sound came hissing louder and sharper, and as he looked towards it, to his alarm Bilbo now saw two small points of light peering at him. As suspicion grew in Gollum's mind, the light of his eyes burned with a pale flame.

"What have you lost?" Bilbo persisted.

But now the light in Gollum's eyes had become a green fire, and it was coming swiftly nearer. Gollum was in his boat again, paddling wildly back to the dark shore; and such a rage of loss and suspicion was in his heart that no sword had any more terror for him.

Bilbo could not guess what had maddened the wretched creature, but he saw that all was up, and that Gollum meant to murder him at any rate. Just in time he turned and ran blindly back up the dark passage down which he had come, keeping close to the wall and feeling it with his left hand.

"What has it got in its pocketses?" he heard the hiss loud behind him, and the splash as Gollum leapt from his boat. "What have I, I wonder?" he said to himself, as he panted and stumbled along. He put his left hand in his pocket. The ring felt very cold as it quietly slipped on to his groping forefinger.

The hiss was close behind him. He turned now and saw Gollum's eyes like small green lamps coming up the slope. Terrified he tried to run faster, but suddenly he struck his toes on a snag in the floor, and fell flat with his little sword under him.

In a moment Gollum was on him. But before Bilbo could do anything, recover his breath, pick himself up, or wave his sword, Gollum passed by, taking no notice of him, cursing and whispering as he ran.

What could it mean? Gollum could see in the dark. Bilbo could see the light of his eyes palely shining even from behind. Painfully he got up, and sheathed his sword, which was now glowing faintly again, then very cautiously he followed. There seemed nothing else to do. It was no good crawling back down to Gollum's water. Perhaps if he followed him, Gollum might lead him to some way of escape without meaning to.

"Curse it! curse it! curse it!" hissed Gollum. "Curse the Baggins! It's gone! What has it got in its pocketses? Oh we guess, we guess, my precious. He's found it, yes he must have. My birthday-present. . . ."

With a spring Gollum got up and started shambling off at a great pace. Bilbo hurried after him, still cautiously, though his chief fear now was of tripping on another snag and falling with a noise. His head was in a whirl of hope and wonder. It seemed that the ring he had was a magic ring: it made you invisible! He had heard of such things, of course, in old old tales; but it was hard to believe that he really had found one, by accident. Still there it was: Gollum with his bright eyes

had passed him by, only a yard to one side.

On they went, Gollum flip-flapping ahead, hissing and cursing; Bilbo behind going as softly as a hobbit can. Soon they came to places where, as Bilbo had noticed on the way down, side-passages opened, this way and that. Gollum began at once to count them.

"One left, yes. One right, yes. Two right, yes, yes. Two left, yes, yes." And so on and on.

As the count grew he slowed down, and he began to get shaky and weepy; for he was leaving the water further and further behind, and he was getting afraid. Goblins might be about, and he had lost his ring. At last he stopped by a low opening, on their left as they went up.

"Seven right, yes. Six left, yes!" he whispered. "This is it. This is the way to the back-door, yes. Here's the passage!"

He peered in, and shrank back. "But we dursn't go in, precious, no we dursn't. Goblinses down there. Lots of goblinses. We smells them. Ssss!

"What shall we do? Curse them and crush them! We must wait here, precious, wait a bit and see."

So they came to a dead stop. Gollum had brought Bilbo to the way out after all, but Bilbo could not get in! There was Gollum sitting humped up right in the opening, and his eyes gleamed cold in his head, as he swayed it from side to side between his knees.

Bilbo almost stopped breathing, and went stiff himself. He was

desperate. He must get away, out of this horrible darkness, while he had any strength left. He must fight. He must stab the foul thing, put its eyes out, kill it. It meant to kill him. No, not a fair fight. he was invisible now. Gollum had no sword. Gollum had not actually threatened to kill him, or tried to yet. And he was miserable, alone, lost. A sudden understanding, a pity mixed with horror, welled up in Bilbo's heart: a glimpse of endless unmarked days without light or hope of betterment, hard stone, cold fish, sneaking and whispering. All these thoughts passed in a flash of a second. He trembled. And then quite suddenly in another flash, as if lifted by a new strength and resolve, he leaped.

No great leap for a man, but a leap in the dark. Straight over Gollum's head he jumped, seven feet forward and three in the air; indeed, had he known it, he only just missed cracking his skull on the low arch of the passage.

Gollum threw himself backwards, and grabbed as the hobbit flew over him, but too late: his hands snapped on thin air, and Bilbo, falling fair on his sturdy feet, sped off down the new tunnel. He did not turn to see what Gollum was doing. There was a hissing and cursing almost at his heels at first, then it stopped. All at once there came a blood-curdling shriek, filled with hatred and despair. Gollum was defeated. He dared go no further. He had lost: lost his prey, and lost, too, the only thing he had ever cared for, his precious. The cry brought Bilbo's heart to his mouth, but still he held on. Now faint as an echo, but menacing, the voice came behind:

"Thief, thief, thief! Baggins! We hates it, we hates it, we hates if for ever!"

Then there was a silence. But that too seemed menacing to Bilbo. "If goblins are so near that he smelt them," he thought, "then they'll have heard his shrieking and cursing. Careful now, or this way will lead you to worse things. . . ."

Scuttling as fast as his legs would carry him he turned the last corner and came suddenly right into an open space, where the light, after all that time in the dark, seemed dazzlingly bright. Really it was only a leak of sunshine in through a doorway, where a great door, a stone door, was left standing open.

Bilbo blinked, and then suddenly he saw the goblins: goblins in full armour with drawn swords sitting just inside the door, and watching it with wide eyes, and watching the passage that led to it. They were aroused, alert, ready for anything.

They saw him sooner than he saw them. Yes, they saw him. Whether it was an accident, or a last trick of the ring before it took a new master, it was not on his finger. With yells of delight the goblins rushed upon him.

A pang of fear and loss, like an echo of Gollum's misery, smote Bilbo, and forgetting even to draw his sword he struck his hands into his pockets. And there was the ring still, in his left pocket, and it slipped on his finger. The goblins stopped short. They could not see a sign of him. He had vanished. They yelled twice as loud as before,

but not so delightedly.

"Where is it?" they cried.

"Go back up the passage! some shouted.

"This way!" some yelled. "That way!" others yelled.

"Look out for the door," bellowed the captain.

Whistles blew, armour clashed, swords rattled, goblins cursed and swore and ran hither and thither, falling over one another and getting very angry. There was a terrible outcry, to-do, and disturbance.

Bilbo was dreadfully frightened, but he had the sense to understand what had happened and to sneak behind a big barrel which held drink for the goblin-guards, and so get out of the way and avoid being bumped into, trampled to death, or caught by feel.

"I must get to the door, I must get to the door!" he kept on saying to himself, but it was a long time before he ventured to try. Then it was like a horrible game of blindman's-buff. The place was full of goblins running about, and the poor little hobbit dodged this way and that, was knocked over by a goblin who could not make out what he had bumped into, scrambled away on all fours, slipped between the legs of the captain just in time, got up, and ran for the door.

It was still ajar, but a goblin had pushed it nearly to. Bilbo struggled but he could not move it. He tried to squeeze through the crack. He squeezed and squeezed, and he stuck! It was awful. His buttons had got wedged on the edge of the door and the door-post. He could see outside into the open air: there were a few steps running down into a

narrow valley between tall mountains: the sun came out from behind a cloud and shone bright on the outside of the door—but he could not get through.

Suddenly one of the goblins inside shouted: "There is a shadow by the door. Something is outside!"

Bilbo's heart jumped into his mouth. He gave a terrific squirm. Buttons burst off in all directions. He was through, with a torn coat and waistcoat, leaping down the steps like a goat, while bewildered goblins were still picking up his nice brass buttons on the doorstep.

Of course they soon came down after him, hooting and halloing, and hunting among the trees. But they don't like the sun: it makes their legs wobble and their heads giddy. They could not find Bilbo with the ring on, slipping in and out of the shadow of the trees, running quick and quiet, and keeping out of the sun; so soon they went back grumbling and cursing to guard the door. Bilbo had escaped.

THE MAGIC GLASS

Guaranteed to amaze everyone at the dinner table.

When no one is looking, hide a match under the tablecloth. Announce your trick, and place the edge of a glass on the match. You can use a glass with liquid in it to make the trick look more dramatic. The match will support the glass at a weird-looking angle.

GRAVEYARD BROWNIES

These magical treats will actually melt in your mouth!

12 Vienna Finger cookies (or other similarly shaped oval cookies)
5 eggs
2 sticks unsalted butter, softened
8 ounces unsweetened chocolate
3 1/2 cups sugar
1 tablespoon pure vanilla extract
1 2/3 cups sifted all-purpose flour
1/2 teaspoon salt

1. Preheat oven to 400° F.
2. Grease a 9 x 13-inch pan.
3. Combine chocolate and butter in a double boiler and heat over simmering water until the mixture is completely melted. Remove from heat and set aside.
4. Beat eggs and sugar with an electric mixer at high speed for 10 minutes. Reduce to low speed and add the melted chocolate and vanilla. Blend well.
5. Add the flour and salt and mix until ingredients are combined.
6. Pour batter into greased pan and bake for 30-35 minutes or until edges are dry but the center is still soft.
7. Remove baking pan from oven and immediately press the Vienna Fingers into the brownies so that they are standing up like gravestones. Make sure you space the cookies evenly so that when you cut the brownies into squares, each piece will have one gravestone/cookie. Allow brownies to cool 20 minutes before cutting and serving. Serve with a large pitcher of milk.

Makes one dozen brownies

The Banshee

One of the most frightening and magical creatures in Irish and Scottish legend is the Banshee. Known as the fairy of death, a visit from the Banshee foretells the certain demise of a family member or loved one. Described as a beautiful young maiden in flowing white robes, the Banshee often delivers her death curse while floating above water or riding upon the back of a galloping steed. Only her crimson eyes betray her inhumanity, for otherwise she looks just like a normal woman. More horrifying than her appearance are the tortured wails and moans she cries out just before the moment of death. So the next time you hear a distant howl, think twice. It could be a neighborhood dog baying at the moon, or it just might be the Banshee coming to pay you a visit.

FRANKENSTEIN

BY MARY SHELLEY

It was on a dreary night of November that I beheld the accomplishment of my toils. With an anxiety that almost amounted to agony, I collected the instruments of life around me, that I might infuse a spark of being into the lifeless thing that lay at my feet. It was already one in the morning; the rain pattered dismally against the panes, and my candle was nearly burnt out, when, by the glimmer of the half-extinguished light, I saw the dull yellow eye of the creature open; it breathed hard, and a convulsive motion agitated it limbs.

How can I describe my emotions at this catastrophe, or how delineate the wretch whom with such infinite pains and care I had endeavoured to form? His limbs were in proportion, and I had selected his features as beautiful. Beautiful! Great God! His yellow skin scarcely covered the work of muscles and arteries beneath; his hair was of a lustrous black, and flowing; his teeth of pearly whiteness; but these luxuriances only formed a more horrid contrast with his watery eyes, that seemed almost of the same colour as the dun-white sockets in which they were set, his shrivelled complexion and straight black lips.

The different accidents of life are not so changeable as the feelings of human nature. I had worked hard for nearly two years, for the sole purpose of infusing life into an inanimate body. For this I had deprived myself of rest and health. I had desired it with an ardour that far exceeded moderation; but now that I had finished, the beauty of the dream vanished, and breathless horror and disgust filled my heart.

The Witches' Chant

Macbeth, Act IV, Scene I

by William Shakespeare

Thunder. Enter the three Witches.

FIRST WITCH

Thrice the brinded cat hath mewed.

SECOND WITCH

Thrice, and once the hedge-pig whined.

THIRD WITCH

Harpier cries "'Tis time, 'tis time!"

FIRST WITCH

Round about the cauldron go;
In the poisoned entrails throw.
Toad, that under cold stone
Days and nights has thirty-one
Sweltered venom sleeping got,
Boil thou first i' th' charmèd pot.

The Witches circle the cauldron.

ALL

Double, double toil and trouble;
Fire burn, and cauldron bubble.

SECOND WITCH

Fillet of a fenny snake
In the cauldron boil and bake.
Eye of newt and toe of frog,
Wool of bat and tongue of dog,
Adder's fork and blindworm's sting,
Lizard's leg and howlet's wing,
For a charm of powerful trouble,
Like a hell-broth boil and bubble.

ALL

Double, double toil and trouble;
Fire burn, and cauldron bubble.

THIRD WITCH

Scale of dragon, tooth of wolf,
Witch's mummy, maw and gulf
Of the ravined salt-sea shark,
Root of hemlock digged i' th' dark,
Liver of blaspheming Jew,
Gall of goat and slips of yew
Slivered in the moon's eclipse,
Nose of Turk and Tartar's lips,
Finger of birth-strangled babe
Ditch-delivered by a drab,
Make the gruel thick and slab.
Add thereto a tiger's chaudron
For th' ingredience of our cauldron.

ALL

Double, double toil and trouble;
Fire burn, and cauldron bubble.

SECOND WITCH

Cool it with a baboon's blood.
Then the charm is firm and good.

Enter Hecate to the other three Witches.

HECATE

O, well done! I commend your pains,
And everyone shall share i' th' gains.
And now about the cauldron sing
Like elves and fairies in a ring,
Enchanting all that you put in.

SECOND WITCH

By the pricking of my thumbs,
Something wicked this way comes.
Open, locks,
Whoever knocks.

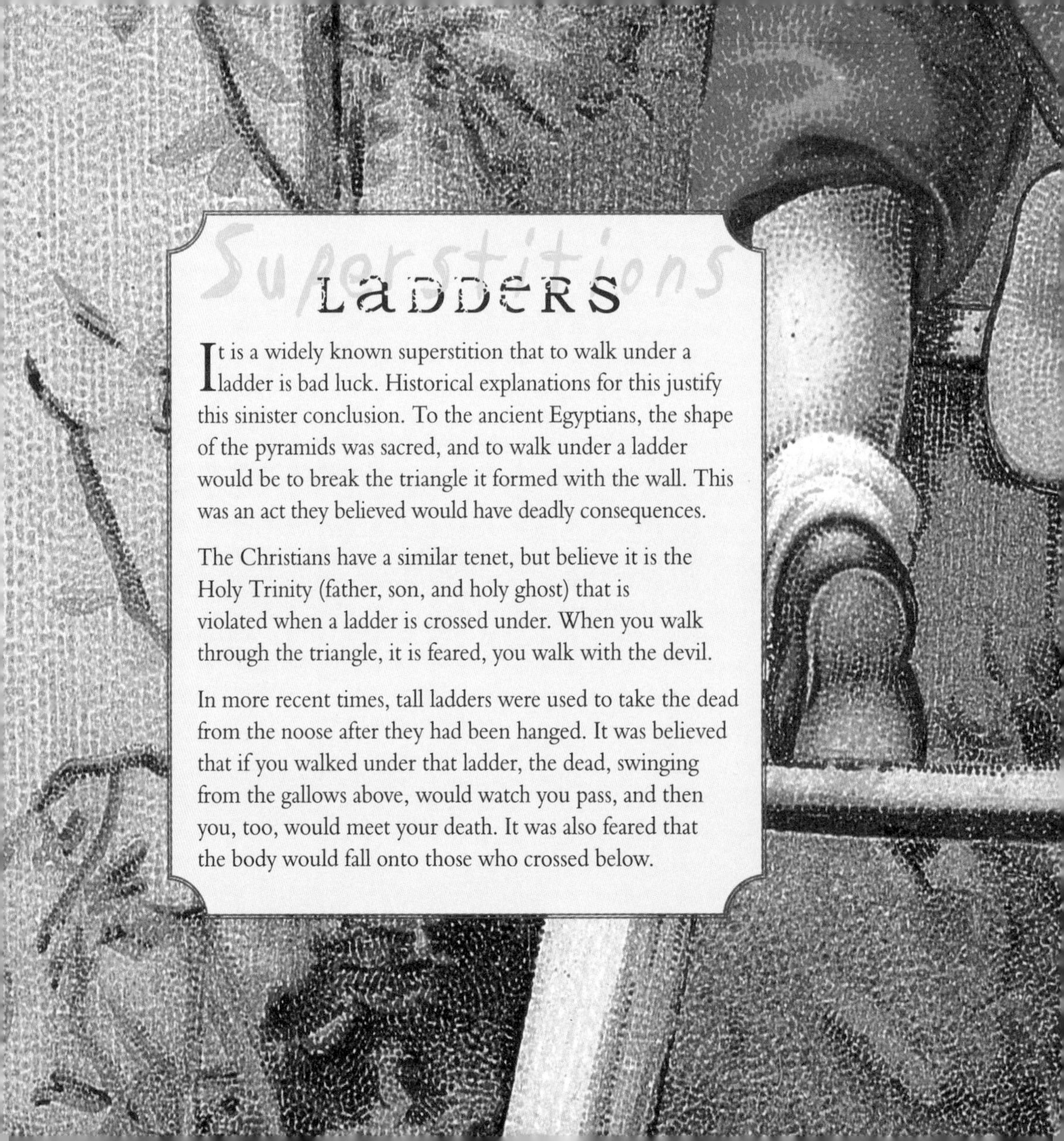

Ladders

It is a widely known superstition that to walk under a ladder is bad luck. Historical explanations for this justify this sinister conclusion. To the ancient Egyptians, the shape of the pyramids was sacred, and to walk under a ladder would be to break the triangle it formed with the wall. This was an act they believed would have deadly consequences.

The Christians have a similar tenet, but believe it is the Holy Trinity (father, son, and holy ghost) that is violated when a ladder is crossed under. When you walk through the triangle, it is feared, you walk with the devil.

In more recent times, tall ladders were used to take the dead from the noose after they had been hanged. It was believed that if you walked under that ladder, the dead, swinging from the gallows above, would watch you pass, and then you, too, would meet your death. It was also feared that the body would fall onto those who crossed below.

THE CURSE OF LADY TICHBORNE

In the year 1150, the saintly Lady Mabella Tichborne lay dying in her room at Tichborne Manor. For months she lacked the strength even to sit by her window and look out over her vast estate, an eden of rich farmland in Hampshire County, England. She summoned her husband, Sir Roger de Tichborne, and shared her dying wish: that a loaf of bread be given to all of the poor once a year on Lady Day, a feast day of the Virgin Mary.

Unlike his wife, greedy Sir Roger felt no compassion for the hungry and quickly schemed to put an end to her request. He told Lady Mabella that he would distribute an annual gift in her name equal to the amount of land she could walk upon holding a lighted torch. Assured that she couldn't get out of bed, the sly Sir Roger felt he'd heard the last of the matter.

But Lady Mabella shocked them all. She crawled out of bed, took the torch, and dragged her skin-and-bones body around 23 acres of the estate. To this day, this parcel of land is known as the Crawls.

Back in her bed, Lady Mabella gathered the household around her and uttered the Tichborne Curse. If the yearly dole of bread was ever stopped, the Tichborne family would die out.

So began the Tichborne Dole, an event that drew vagrants, gypsies, and other poor British inhabitants to Hampshire County every year on March 25th. The custom went on for 600 years, until the local government got fed up with the influx of riff-raff and shut it down in 1794. As a result, male Tichborne heirs began to die.

Edward Doughty, a Tichborne who had changed his name, realized the curse was in action when four of his brothers died without children. With the sudden death of his six-year-old son—the only remaining Tichborne heir—he reinstated the dole, which has been handed out ever since. Today, families from the neighborhood gather at Tichborne Manor on Lady Day with buckets, bags and pillowcases to collect a few pounds of flour sprinkled with holy water.

A Spell to
Scare Away
A Monster

Here's a handy spell to get rid of any monsters or boogey men who may be lurking under the bed or in the closet.

Before going to sleep, flick the bedroom light switch on and off thirteen times while reciting the following charm:

> Monsters lurking far and near,
> Your jaws of death I do not fear.
>
> There are no children sleeping here,
> So scamper off and disappear!

The Troll

by Ray Bradbury

Once upon a time, when wishing wasn't having, there was an old man who lived under a bridge. He lived there for as long as people remembered.

"I'm a troll," he said.

When people passed on the bridge above he cried out, "Who goes there?"

When they told him, he would demand, "Where going?"

And when they had outlined their destination, he would say, "Are you a good, kind person?'

And when they said, "Oh, yes," he would let them pass.

He got to be quite a character with the people up in the village who said, "Go visit the troll. Don't be afraid. His bark is worse than his bite. He's much fun when you get to know him."

On summer days the children would hang over the stone rim of the bridge and call down into the cool spaces, "Troll, troll, troll." And the echoes would blow up cool and clear, "Troll, troll, troll. . . ." And then they saw his reflection in the slow running water, a wry, old face with a twisty green beard woven of moss and fresh reeds, it seemed, with green moss eyebrows and pointed wax-white ears. His fingers

were horny and clawed and his naked body was clothed with reeds and green grass and verdigris, wet and gleaming.

And his reflection in the water would call back up to them. "What do you want?"

"Some crayfish, troll."

"Some snails, troll."

Some tadpoles, troll."

"Some bright stones, troll."

And if they went away a while and didn't look, when they came back they would find some delicate, scuttling crayfish placed upon the bridge rail, along with some slow snails, a few wriggling tadpoles, and some bright pink and blue-white stones from the deepest part of the creek.

"Oh, thank you, troll."

"Thank you, thank you, thank you, troll," the child voices would call into the green coolness, into the water shadows.

Drip, drip went the water. No answer. The water slid under the bridge in the summertime, and the children went on their way.

But one summer day, as the troll was basking at his ease beneath the bridge, listening to the water purl between his soaking hooves, his eyes shut and at rest, he heard a great horning and tooting and something banged over the bridge above.

"One of those idiots with his new car," murmured the troll.

"Damn fool, when he could be down here, in the water shadows all summer, watching the light on the stream, feeling it slide by with your hand or your hoof. Such rushing fools up there in that hot world!"

Not a minute later he heard two people pass on the bridge. By the tread of their shoes he knew it to be two men, and one of them was saying, "Did you see that red Jaguar? Boy, was he traveling!"

"Know who that was? Our fruitcake psychiatrist! You see his new office, most modern building downtown? He's come to get us nuts off the tree, cure our neuroses, put us back on the tree, or so he said on TV last night."

"Well, well," said the other. "He sure advertises! That car's a fire engine!"

"Believes in expression, no frustrations, so he said, loud and clear."

The voices passed.

The troll, listening idly, eyes shut, was only faintly stirred by the conversation. There was a nice long summer ahead, here in this midwestern town, and then when winter froze the stream to milk-glass, he would float south leisurely, like a clump of moss and reed, easing down toward the sea, to spend a few months in a creek under a bridge in the spring. It was not a bad life at all, one had one's perambulating stations, people respected you, and on occasion (here he licked his lips) you met up with a scoundrel, a thief, some perpetual criminal, and the world thanked you for services offered and services rendered. He

thought of himself as a sieve hunkered here to strain the light and dark civilizations that passed above. He could guess the pace of murdering thieves forty paces away. None of them would last through an idling and suddenly violent summer.

This train of thought sat him up, musing. "Why," he wondered, "hasn't there been a really bad one through all June or July? Here it's getting almost August and I've had to make do on mini-frogs and crayfish. A frugal lunch, no dinner at all. Where, oh where is the dark flesh and rancid blood of a true, fat-traveling villain?"

Hardly had he finished this half-prayer than he heard a sound of voices far off, and quick footsteps, a very defiant series of footsteps, hurrying down the road.

"I wouldn't go near there, if I were you," warned a woman's voice.

"Bosh!" a man said. "I'll find this so-called troll myself. I don't need your help."

"So-called troll?" The troll stiffened. He waited.

A moment later, a head popped over the rim of the bridge. A pair of beady black licorice eyes stared wildly down.

"Troll!" yelled the strange man. "You *there*!?"

Troll almost plunged into the water. He lurched back into the cool shadows.

"Is *that* what they call you, the damn-fool villagers here?" the stranger above wondered. "Or did you make the name up so you could blackmail pedestrians and grab their cash?"

Troll was so stunned, his mouth froze.

"Come on, speak up, come out, the game's up, cut the comedy!" shouted the stranger.

At last, Troll inched over and glared up at the loud man suspended in the noon glare.

"And who," muttered Troll, are you?"

"I'm Dr. Crowley. Psychiatrist. Eminent. That's who," snapped the loud man, his face crimson from hanging upside down. "And since this is a very undignified posture, why don't you come up in the sunlight? Let's talk man to man."

"I have nothing to discuss with you, Dr. Crowley." The troll subsided against the bank below.

"Then, at least," barked the psychiatrist, "give me your name!"

"Troll."

The doctor snapped his fingers. "Come, come! Don't be ridiculous! Your *real* name!"

"Well, *Summer Bridge* Troll . . . or Green Moss Summer Bridge Troll, should you want the whole thing."

"When did this first come over you?" asked the irritable doctor.

"What?"

"To sit under *bridges*. When you were a child?"

"I've *always* sat under bridges."

"I see." The face vanished. Above, a pen scratched. A voice murmured, "*Always* sat under bridges. So." The face reappeared, perspiring. "Did you run away from home often, away from siblings?"

"Siblings!?" cried the troll, confused, "what in hell's that? I never *had* a home."

"Ah." The face vanished again. The voice murmured, the pen scraped. "Orphan. Psychologically dispossessed." Like a stringless puppet the doctor thrust himself down. "What would you say attracted you *most* about bridges. The shadows, the secrecy, eh? The stashed-away element, yes? Right?"

"No," said the troll, irritably, "I simply like it here."

"Like!" cried the psychiatrist. "There's no such thing as 'like.' Every thing has *roots*! You are probably suffering from a back-to-the-womb complex. Societal withdrawal. Paranoia. Leader complex. Yes, that's *it*! You hide down here and holler up at anyone who passes. Oh, I know about you. That's one reason why I came. I traveled a long way to investigate you and the people of this village with their superstitions. But especially, *you*!"

"Me?"

"Yes, the word spread there was a troll in residence who asks each fool crossing, 'are you passing good or loping evil?'"

"What's wrong with that?" demanded Troll.

"My dear fellow, everyone knows there is no dichotomy of bad and good. It's all relative."

"Sorry," said Troll, "I don't see it that way."

"Did you ever consider environment as a factor when you asked people if they were good or evil?"

Troll snorted peevishly.

"Or heredity. Do you research the genetics of the people you supposedly eat? You *do* eat people?"

"I do."

"Tut! You only *think* you do. That's an extension of your preoccupation with curing people of their so-called sins. You imagine that by snacking on them you can digest their crimes. What you do, however, is convince yourself that each time a local thief vanishes, you have dined off his bones."

"*Haven't* I?"

"No comment. Now, how long have you lurked down there?"

"One hundred years."

"Poppycock. You're seventy at most. When were you born?"

"I was never born. I just grew. Some reeds, some crayfish, snails, grass, lots of moss, fermented, coagulated, here in the rock's shade a century back, and here I was."

"Highly fanciful but hardly of any help to me," the psychiatrist declared.

"Who asked you to come here?"

"Well, truthfully, I came on my own. You lured me as a neurotic manifestation within a culture."

"You mean to hang up there and tell me I haven't done a good job, doc?!" Troll shouted so the echoes roared. "you came to make me doubt my work, make me unhappy, yes?!"

"No, no, I came simply to help you to arise and flourish, so you can live in this world and be happy."

"I *am* happy! I *am* content. Go!"

"You only think you are. I'll come to interview you each day until we solve your problem."

"The problem is yours." Troll quivered. His hooves flinted the rocks. "A year ago, doctor, a very bad man, a man who shot and robbed people, crossed the bridge. I said, are you good or evil, and thinking I wouldn't guess he told the truth, he laughingly said, evil. An instant later the bridge was empty as I sat down to dine. Now, do you mean to tell me I erred in flaying and deboning that man?"

"What, without researching his life, to scan his love-starved youth, his starved ego, his need for love, for comfort and help?"

"I loved him immensely. I helped myself to *him*. What if I told you I've breakfasted on ten hundred such men in my lifetime, doctor?" asked the troll.

"I'd say you were an obsessional liar."

"What if I proved it?"

"Then? You'd be a murder."

"Good or evil?"

"What?"

"A good or an evil murdered, Doctor Crowley?"

The doctor's face dripped sweat. "It's awfully hot here in the sun."

"Your cheeks *are* red. how old are you, Crowley? Look like a heart case. Better not hang there too long with your scratch-pad. Answer my question. Am I a good or evil killer?"

"Neither! Yours was a lonely childhood. Obviously, you retreated here years ago, to set yourself up as the town's moral tyrant."

"Did the town complain?"

Silence

"*Did* it?"

"No."

"They're satisfied to have me here, yes?"

"That's not the question."

"*They're* satisfied. They didn't send for you."

"You need me," said Dr. Crowley.

"Yes, I guess I do," said the troll at last.

"You *admit* it?"

"I do."

"You'll take my treatments?"

"Yes." The troll lay back in the shadows.

The doctor's face perspired in excess as his face blushed. "Glorious! Oh, but, god, it's hot!"

His spectacles blazed with sunlight.

"Fool," whispered the troll. "Why do you think I stay here? It's

icehouse cool on the hottest day. Come down."

The psychiatrist hesitated.

"I believe I will," he said, finally. "Just for a moment."

His feet slid over the edge of the bridge.

In the late afternoon, three children passed above.

"Troll, troll," they called.

"Troll, troll," they sang.

"Troll, troll, troll."

"Give us a stone, give us a shell, give us a frog. Troll, troll, give us a gift, give us a nice gift, troll."

They walked off and then turned back.

And there, dripping in the little pool of cool water on the stone rim of the bridge, lay a shell, a tadpole, a fountain pen, a pad, and a pair of bright silver-rimmed spectacles.

The stream went under the bridge silently. And as they bent to call "Troll, troll!" they saw something that resembled a lazy cool mass of green reed and green grass and green moss float slowly and slowly south and south in the tide, even as the skies clouded and birds circled and the first smell of autumn touched the air. ☾

ALL SOUL'S DAY BREAD

3 packages dry yeast
4 cups lukewarm water
1 tablespoon white sugar
5 eggs (preferably room temperature)
3 sticks melted butter
2 cupped handfuls of kosher salt
1/2 cup honey
1/4-1/2 cup of molasses
9 cups whole wheat flour
6 cups unbleached white flour

1. Preheat oven to 450°F and grease and flour 5 bread pans.
2. Pour yeast into 2 cups of the water with a tablespoon of sugar. Let sit in a warmish place for 15-20 minutes until it gets all foamy.
3. Add eggs, butter, salt, honey, molasses, the other 2 cups of water and the whole-wheat flour.
4. Blend well, then add most of the white flour and mix again. Let stand 5 minutes.
5. Turn out on to a floured board or table. Knead for 10-15 minutes.
6. Put dough into a large buttered bowl and turn over a few times until all sides are covered with butter. Cover with a damp dishtowel. Put it in a warm place (over radiator, near stove, etc.).
7. Leave for 1 1/2-2 hours while dough rises to double its original size. Punch it down and leave to rise again (another 1/2 hour or so).
8. Turn on to floured board again. Cut dough into five pieces and knead each one before shaping it. Put into bread pans and let rise one more time.
9. Bake bread for 10 minutes, then decrease temperature to 350°F for another 30 minutes or until the top of the bread is a rich, dark brown.

Makes 5 loaves

THE GHOSTLY MARK

This tricks makes a letter magically appear on the hand of someone in your audience.

Using a black magic marker, draw the letter "G" for Ghost on a sugar cube.

Secretly press your index finger on the G so that it leaves a mark.

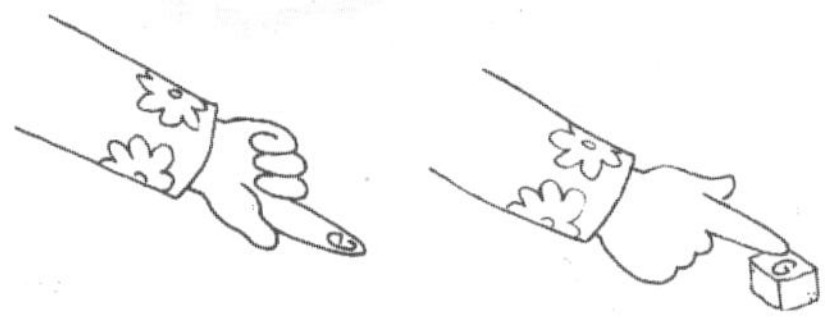

Drop the sugar cube into a glass of water, saying "Melt, magical sugar, and make your sign appear somewhere in this room!"

Ask a friend to put his/her hand over the glass. Take the person's hand and press your index finger into her palm as you hold it.

Tell your friend to take her hand away and lift her palm. The ghost's signature "G" appears for everyone to see!

Merlin

In early Celtic tales Merlin was a poet, a prophet, a magician and a sage. At times he was also a hermit—at other times a conjurer and wizard.

It is believed that the myth of Merlin originated in the character of a Northern Welshman named Myrddin-or the madman and prophet of Scottish legend, Lailoken. He is believed to have caused the Battle of Arderydd in the 570s by provoking the British chieftains. As supernatural punishment, he lost his mind and was seen wandering the forests of Celidon in the Scottish lowlands.

But it is the story of King Arthur that turned Merlin into a true legend. As the sorcerer and court wizard who was Arthur's most important advisor, Merlin dwelled in enchanted places and used magic to manipulate nature. His powers of wizardry embraced both darkness and light (unlike his half-sister Morgan le Fay, a fairy witch, used her magical powers only to do evil). Merlin could change into a stag or a boy or any other creature, depending on his surroundings. He could also change others and make them invisible.

According to lore, King Uther was in love with Lady Ingraine, wife of the Duke of Tintagel. When she refused his advances, he called on Merlin for help. Using his powers, Merlin transformed Uther so he appeared to Ingraine as her own husband, and later Arthur was born. In exchange, Merlin asked the king to let him educate Arthur. So began the long relationship between Merlin and Arthur. The wizard trained Arthur as a knight and helped him prove himself and ascend the throne by giving him the sword in the stone. It was also Merlin who warned Arthur that the copper-haired beauty Guinevere would bring about his doom.

Later, Merlin himself fell for Nimue, Lady of the Lake. He proclaimed his love for her, but she was frightened and resisted him. Merlin made a spell to bind her to his side. Fearing his strength, the lake spirit begged him to teach her the secrets of his magic. He reluctantly agreed and led her to a silvery cave, where she put a spell on him that he himself had taught her. Merlin fell into a deep sleep and was imprisoned in the cave for eternity.

The Magic Shop

by H. G. Wells

I had seen the Magic Shop from afar several times; I had passed it once or twice, a shop window of alluring little objects, magic balls, magic hens, wonderful cones, ventriloquist dolls, the material of the basket trick, packs of cards that *looked* all right, and all that sort of thing, but never had I thought of going in until one day, almost without warning, Gip hauled me by my finger right up to the window, and so conducted himself that there was nothing for it but to take him in.

"If I was rich," said Gip, dabbling a finger at the Disappearing Egg, "I'd buy myself that. And that"—which was The Crying Baby, Very Human—"and that," which was a mystery, and called, so a neat card asserted, "Buy One and Astonish your Friends."

"Anything," said Gip, "will disappear under one of those cones. I have read about it in a book.

"And there, dadda, is the Vanishing Halfpenny—only they've put it this way up so's we can't see how it's done."

Gip, dear boy, inherits his mother's breeding, and he did not propose to enter the shop or worry in any way; only, you know, quite unconsciously he lugged my finger doorward, and he made his interest clear.

"That," he said, and pointed to the Magic Bottle.

"If you had that?" I said; at which promising inquiry he looked up with a sudden radiance.

"I could show it to Jessie," he said, thoughtful as ever of others.

"It's less than a hundred days to your birthday, Gibbles," I said, and laid my hand on the door-handle.

Gip made no answer, but his grip tightened on my finger, and so we came into the shop.

It was no common shop this; it was a magic shop, and all the prancing precedence Gip would have taken in the matter of mere toys was wanting. He left the burthen of the conversation to me.

It was a little, narrow shop, not very well lit, and the door-bell pinged again with a plaintive note as we closed it behind us. For a moment or so we were alone and could glance about us. There was a tiger in *papier-mâché* on the glass case that covered the low counter—a grave, kind-eyed tiger that waggled his head in a methodical manner; there were several crystal spheres, a china hand holding magic cards, a stock of magic fish-bowls in various sizes, and an immodest magic hat that shamelessly displayed its springs. On the floor were magic mirrors; one to draw you out long and thin, one to swell your head and vanish your legs, and one to make you short and fat like a draught; and while we were laughing at these the shopman, as I suppose, came in.

At any rate, there he was behind the counter—a curious, sallow,

dark man, with one ear larger than the other and a chin like the toe-cap of a boot.

"What can we have the pleasure?" he said, spreading his long, magic fingers on the glass case; and so with a start we were aware of him.

"I want," I said, "to buy my little boy a few simple tricks."

"Legerdemain?" he asked. "Mechanical? Domestic?"

"Anything amusing?" said I.

"Um!" said the shopman, and scratched his head for a moment as if thinking. Then, quite distinctly, he drew from his head a glass ball. "Something is this way?" he said, and held it out.

The action was unexpected. I had seen the trick done at entertainments endless times before—it's part of the common stock of conjurers—but I had not expected it here. "That's good," I said, with a laugh.

"Isn't it?" said the shopman.

Gip stretched out his disengaged hand to take this object and found merely a blank palm.

"It's in your pocket," said the shopman, and there it was!

"How much will that be?" I asked.

"We make no charge for glass balls," said the shopman, politely. "We get them"—he picked one out of his elbow as he spoke—"free." He produced another from the back of his neck, and laid it beside its predecessor on the counter. Gip regarded his glass ball sagely, then directed a look of inquiry at the two on the counter, and finally brought his round-eyed scrutiny to the shopman, who smiled. "You may have

those too," said the shopman, "and if you don't mind, one from my mouth—*So!*"

Gip counselled me mutely for a moment, and then in a profound silence put away the four balls, resumed my reassuring finger, and nerved himself for the next event.

"We get all our smaller tricks in that way," the shopman remarked.

I laughed in the manner of one who subscribes to a jest. "Instead of going to the wholesale shop," I said. "Of course, it's cheaper."

"In a way," the shopman said. "Though we pay in the end. But not so heavily—as people suppose. . . . Our larger tricks and our daily provisions and all the other things we want, we get out of that hat. . . . And you know, sir, if you'll excuse my saying it, there isn't a wholesale shop, not for Genuine Magic goods, sir. I don't know if you noticed our inscription—the Genuine Magic shop." He drew a business-card from his cheek and handed it to me. "Genuine," he said, with his finger on the word, and added, "There is absolutely no deception, sir."

He seemed to be carrying out the joke pretty thoroughly, I thought.

He turned to Gip with a smile of remarkable affability. "You, you know, are the Right Sort of Boy."

I was surprised at his knowing that, because, in the interests of discipline, we keep it rather a secret even at home; but Gip received it in unflinching silence, keeping a steadfast eye on him.

"It's only the Right Sort of Boy gets through that doorway."

And as if by way of illustration, there came a rattling at the door, and a squeaking little voice could be faintly heard. "Nyar! I *warn* 'a go in there dadda, I WARN 'a go in there. Nya-a-a-ah!" and then the accents of a down-trodden parent urging consolations and propitiations. "It's locked, Edward," he said.

"But it isn't," said I.

"It is, sir," said the shopman, "always—for that sort of child," and as he spoke we had a glimpse of the other youngster, a small, white face, pallid from sweet-eating and over-sapid food, and distorted by evil passions, a ruthless little egotist, pawing at the enchanted pane. "It's no good, sir," said the shopman, as I moved, with my natural helpfulness, doorward, and presently the spoilt child was carried off howling.

"How do you manage that?" I said, breathing more freely.

"Magic!" said the shopman, with a careless wave of the hand, and behold! sparks of coloured fire flew out of his fingers and vanished into the shadows of the shop.

"You were saying," he said, addressing himself to Gip, "before you came in, that you would like one of our 'Buy One and Astonish your Friends' boxes?"

Gip, after a gallant effort, said "Yes."

"It's in your pocket."

And leaning over the counter—he really had an extraordinarily long body—this amazing person produced the article in the customary conjurer's manner. "Paper," he said, and took a sheet out of the empty hat with the springs: "string," and behold his mouth was a string-box, from which he drew an unending thread, which when he had tied his parcel he bit off—and, it seemed to me, swallowed the ball of string. And then he lit a candle at the nose of one of the ventriloquist's dummies, stuck one of his fingers (which had become sealing-wax red) into the flame, and so sealed the parcel. "Then there was the Disappearing Egg," he remarked, and produced one from within my coat-breast and packed it, and also The Crying Baby, Very Human. I handed each parcel to Gip as it was ready, and he clasped them to his chest.

He said very little, but his eyes were eloquent; the clutch of his arms was eloquent. He was the playground of unspeakable emotions. These, you know, were *real* Magics.

Then, with a start, I discovered something moving about in my hat—something soft and jumpy. I whipped it off, and a ruffled pigeon—no doubt a confederate—dropped out and ran on the counter, and went, I fancy, into a cardboard box behind the *papier-mâché* tiger.

"Tut, tut!" said the shopman, dexterously relieving me of my headdress; "careless bird, and—as I live—nesting!"

He shook my hat, and shook out into his extended hand two or three eggs, a large marble, a watch, about half-a-dozen of the inevitable glass balls, and the crumpled, crinkled paper, more and more and more, talking all the time of the way in which people neglect to brush their hats *inside* as well as out, politely, of course, but with a certain personal application. "All sorts of things accumulate, sir. . . . Not *you*, of course, in particular. . . . Nearly every customer. . . . Astonishing what they carry about with them. . . ." The crumpled paper rose and billowed on the counter more and more and more, until he was nearly hidden from us, until he was altogether hidden, and still his voice went on and on. "We none of us know what the fair semblance of a human being may conceal, sir. Are we all then no better than brushed exteriors, whited sepulchres—"

His voice stopped—exactly like when you hit a neighbour's gramophone with a well-aimed brick, the same instant silence, and the rustle of the paper stopped, and everything was still. . . .

"Have you done with my hat?" I said, after an interval.

There was no answer.

I stared at Gip, and Gip stared at me, and there were our distortions in the magic mirrors, looking very run, and grave, and quiet. . . .

"I think we'll go now," I said. "Will you tell me how much all this comes to? . . .

"I say," I said, on a rather louder note, "I want the bill; and my hat, please."

It might have been a sniff from behind the paper pile....

"Let's look behind the counter, Gip," I said. "He's making fun of us."

I led Gip round the head-wagging tiger, and what do you think there was behind the counter? No one at all! Only my hat on the floor, and a common conjurer's lop-eared white rabbit lost in meditation, and looking as stupid and crumpled as only a conjurer's rabbit can do. I resumed my hat, and the rabbit lolloped a lollop or so out of my way.

"Dadda!" said Gip, in a guilty whisper.

"What is it, Gip?" said I.

"I *do* like this shop, dadda."

"So should I," I said to myself, "if the counter wouldn't suddenly extend itself to shut one off from the door." But I didn't call Gip's attention to that. "Pussy!" he said, with a hand out to the rabbit as it came lolloping past us; "Pussy, do Gip a magic!" and his eyes followed it as it squeezed through a door I had certainly not remarked a moment before. Then this door opened wider, and the man with one ear larger than the other appeared again. He was smiling still, but his eye met mine with something between amusement and defiance. "You'd like to see our showroom, sir," he said, with an innocent suavity. Gip tugged my finger forward. I glanced at the counter and met the shopman's eye again. I was beginning to think the magic just a little too genuine. "We haven't very much time," I said. But somehow we were inside the showroom before I could finish that.

"All goods of the same quality," said the shopman, rubbing his flexible hands together, "and that is the Best. Nothing in the place that isn't genuine Magic, and warranted thoroughly rum. Excuse me, sir!"

I felt him pull at something that clung to my coat-sleeve, and then I saw he held a little, wriggling red demon by the tail—the little creature bit and fought and tried to get at his hand—and in a moment he tossed it carelessly behind a counter. No doubt the thing was only an image of twisted indiarubber, but for the moment—! And his gesture was exactly that of a man who handles some petty biting bit of vermin. I glanced at Gip, but Gip was looking at a magic rocking horse. I was glad he hadn't seen the thing. "I say," I said, in an undertone, and indicating Gip and the red demon with my eyes, "you haven't many things like *that* about, have you?"

"None of ours! Probably brought it with you," said the shopman—also in an undertone, and with a more dazzling smile than ever. "Astonishing what people *will* carry about with them unawares!" And then to Gip, "Do you see anything you fancy here?"

There were many things that Gip fancied there.

He turned to this astonishing tradesman with mingled confidence and respect. "Is that a Magic Sword?" he said.

"A Magic Toy Sword. It neither bends, breaks, nor cuts the fingers. It renders the bearer invincible in battle against anyone under eighteen. Half-a-crown to seven and sixpence, according to size. These panoplies on cards are for juvenile knights-errant and very useful—

shield of safety, sandals of swiftness, helmet of invisibility."

"Oh, dadda!" gasped Gip.

I tried to find out what they cost, but the shopman did not heed me. He had got Gip now; he had got him away from my finger; he had embarked upon the exposition of all his confounded stock, and nothing was going to stop him. Presently I saw with a qualm of distrust and something very like jealousy that Gip had hold of this person's finger as usually he has hold of mine. No doubt the fellow was interesting, I thought, and had an interestingly faked lot of stuff, really *good* faked stuff, still—

I wandered after them, saying very little, but keeping an eye on this prestidigital fellow. After all, Gip was enjoying it. And no doubt when the time came to go we should be able to go quite easily.

It was a long, rambling place, that showroom, a gallery broken up by stands and stalls and pillars, with archways leading off to other departments, in which the queerest-looking assistants loafed and stared at one, and with perplexing mirrors and curtains. So perplexing, indeed, were these that I was presently unable to make out the door by which we had come.

The shopman showed Gip magic trains that ran without steam or clockwork, just as you set the signals, and then some very, very valuable boxes of soldiers that all came alive directly you took off the lid and said—I myself haven't a very quick ear and it was a tongue-twisting sound, but Gip—he has his mother's ear—got it in no time. "Bravo!"

said the shopman, putting the men back into the box unceremoniously and handing it to Gip. "Now," said the shopman, and in a moment Gip had made them all alive again.

"You'll take that box?" asked the shopman.

"We'll take that box," said I, "unless you charge its full value. In which case it would need a Trust Magnate—"

"Dear heart! *No!*" and the shopman swept the little men back again, shut the lid, waved the box in the air, and there it was, in brown paper, tied up and—*with Gip's full name and address on the paper!*

The shopman laughed at my amazement.

"This is the genuine magic," he said. "The real thing."

"It's almost too genuine for my taste," I said again.

After that he fell to showing Gip tricks, odd tricks, and still odder the way they were done. He explained them, he turned them inside out, and there was the dear little chap nodding his busy bit of a head in the sagest manner.

I did not attend as well as I might. "Hey, presto!" said the Magic Shopman, and then would come the clear, small "Hey, presto!" of the boy. But I was distracted by other things. It was being borne in upon me just how tremendously rum this place was; it was, so to speak, inundated by a sense of rumness. There was something vaguely rum about the fixtures even, about the ceiling, about the floor, about the casually distributed chairs. I had a queer feeling that whenever I wasn't looking at them straight they went askew, and moved about, and played a

noiseless puss-in-the-corner behind my back. And the cornice had a serpentine design with masks—masks altogether too expressive for proper plaster.

Then abruptly my attention was caught by one of the odd-looking assistants. He was some way off and evidently unaware of my presence—I saw a sort of three-quarter length of him over a pile of toys and through an arch—and, you know, he was leaning against a pillar in an idle sort of way doing the most horrid things with his features! The particularly horrid thing he did was with his nose. He did it just as though he was idle and wanted to amuse himself. First of all it was a short, blobby nose, and then suddenly he shot it out like a telescope, and then out it flew and became thinner and thinner until it was like a long, red, flexible whip. Like a thing in a nightmare it was! He flourished it about and flung it forth as a fly-fisher flings his line.

My instant thought was that Gip mustn't see him. I turned about, and there was Gip quite preoccupied with the shopman, and thinking no evil. They were whispering together and looking at me. Gip was standing on a stool, and the shopman was holding a sort of big drum in his hand.

"Hide and seek, dadda!" cried Gip. "You're He!"

And before I could do anything to prevent it, the shopman had clapped the big drum over him.

I saw what was up directly. "Take that off," I cried, "this instant! You'll frighten the boy. Take it off!"

The shopman with the unequal ears did so without a word, and held the big cylinder towards me to show its emptiness. And the stool was vacant! In that instant my boy had utterly disappeared! . . .

You know, perhaps, that sinister something that comes like a hand out of the unseen and grips your heart about. You know it takes your common self away and leaves you tense and deliberate, neither slow nor hasty, neither angry nor afraid. So it was with me.

I came up to this grinning shopman and kicked his stool aside.

"Stop this folly!" I said. "Where is my boy?"

"You see," he said, still displaying the drum's interior, "there is no deception—"

I put out my hand to grip him, and he eluded me by a dexterous movement. I snatched again, and he turned from me and pushed open a door to escape. "Stop!" I said, and he laughed, receding. I leapt after him—into utter darkness.

Thud!

"Lor' bless my 'eart! I didn't see you coming, sir!"

I was in Regent Street, and I had collided with a decent-looking working man; and a yard away, perhaps, and looking extremely perplexed with himself, was Gip. There was some sort of apology, and

then Gip had turned and come to me with a bright little smile, as though for a moment he had missed me.

And he was carrying four parcels in his arm!

He secured immediate possession of my finger.

For the second I was rather at a loss. I stared round to see the door of the magic shop, and, behold, it was not there! There was no door, no shop, nothing, only the common pilaster between the shop where they sell pictures and the window with the chicks! . . .

I did the only thing possible in that mental tumult; I walked straight to the kerbstone and held up my umbrella for a cab.

"'Ansoms," said Gip, in a note of culminating exultation.

I helped him in, recalled my address with an effort, and got in also. Something unusual proclaimed itself in my tail-coat pocket, and I felt and discovered a glass ball. With a petulant expression I flung it into the street.

Gip said nothing.

For a space neither of us spoke.

"Dadda!" said Gip, at last, "that *was* a proper shop!"

I came round with that to the problem of just how the whole thing had seemed to him. He looked completely undamaged—so far, good; he was neither scared nor unhinged, he was simply tremendously satisfied with the afternoon's entertainment, and there in his arms were the four parcels.

Confound it! what could be in them?

"Um!" I said. "Little boys can't go to shops like that every day."

He received this with his usual stoicism, and for a moment I was sorry I was his father and not his mother, and so couldn't suddenly there, *coram publico*, in our hansom, kiss him. After all, I thought, the thing wasn't so very bad.

But it was only when we opened the parcels that I really began to be reassured. Three of them contained boxes of soldiers, quite ordinary lead soldiers, but of so good a quality as to make Gip altogether forget that originally these parcels had been Magic Tricks of the only genuine sort, and the fourth contained a kitten, a little living white kitten, in excellent health and appetite and temper.

I saw this unpacking with a sort of provisional relief. I hung about in the nursery for quite an unconscionable time. . . .

That happened six months ago. And now I am beginning to believe it is all right. The kitten had only the magic natural to all kittens, and the soldiers seem as steady a company as any colonel could desire. And Gip—?

The intelligent parent will understand that I have to go cautiously with Gip.

But I went so far as this one day. I said, "How would you like your soldiers to come alive, Gip, and march about by themselves?"

"Mine do," said Gip. "I just have to say a word I know before I open the lid."

"Then they march about alone?"

"Oh, *quite*, dadda. I shouldn't like them if they didn't do that."

I displayed no unbecoming surprise, and since then I have taken occasion to drop in upon him once or twice, unannounced, when the soldiers were about, but so far I have never discovered them performing in anything like a magical manner. . . .

It's so difficult to tell.

There's also a question of finance. I have an incurable habit of paying bills. I have been up and down Regent Street several times, looking for that shop. I am inclined to think, indeed, that in that matter honour is satisfied, and that, since Gip's name and address are known to them, I may very well leave it to these people, whoever they may be, to send in their bill in their own time. ☾

THE FLOATING FRIEND

They've seen it on TV, but you can bring it to their very eyes.

You'll need two sticks that are tall enough to reach from the floor to the neck of your magic show assistant.

Put a pair of shoes on the end of the sticks. Your friend straddles a bench and leans back until his head is resting on the bench. He holds the sticks along his sides. You have covered him with a sheet so the shoes on the end of the sticks stick out on one side and his head on the other.

You wave your magic wand or use your arms to cast a magic spell, motioning him to rise.

Your partner slowly stands up, holding the sticks straight out the entire time. With the sheet covering him, it looks like his whole body is rising from the bench.

Transylvania Dreaming

by Colin McNaughton

In the middle of the night
When you're safe in bed
And the doors are locked
And the cats are fed
And it's much too bright
And sleep won't come
And there's something wrong
And you want your mom
And you hear a noise
And you see a shape
And it looks like a bat
Or a man in a cape
And you dare not breathe
And your heart skips a beat
And you're cold as ice
From your head to your feet
And you say a prayer
And you swear to be good
And you'd run for your life

If you only could
And your eyes are wide
And stuck on stalks
As the thing in black
Toward you walks
And the room goes dark
And you faint clean away
And you don't wake up
Till the very next day . . .

And you open your eyes
And the sun is out
And you jump out of bed
And you sing and shout,
"It was only a dream!"
And you dance around the room
And your heart is as light
As a helium balloon
And your mom rushes in
And says, "Hold on a sec . .

What are those two little
Holes in your neck?"

SPIDER CAKE

Simple and delicious. Make one large chocolate spider web or little ones on the corners of the orange frosting!

Cake
2 large eggs
2/3 cup sugar
2/3 cup butter
2 teaspoons grated orange rind
3/4 cup sifted cake flour
3/4 teaspoons baking powder
1/4 teaspoon salt

1. Preheat oven to 325°F.
2. Grease one 8-inch layer cake pan and dust with fine, dry breadcrumbs.
3. Mix eggs and sugar until light and fluffy.
4. Cream butter with orange rind.
5. In a large bowl, combine flour, baking powder, and salt. Add egg and butter mixtures and blend well with flour mixture.
6. Spoon batter into pan and bake for about 25-30 minutes, or until a toothpick inserted into the center comes out clean.
7. Cool cake in pan for 10 minutes. Remove from pan and cool completely before icing.

Frosting
1 cup confectioners' sugar
2 tablespoons concentrated orange juice
2 squares of milk or dark chocolate

1. Mix sugar and juice until smooth.
2. Spread over top and sides of cooled cake.
3. Put 2 squares of milk or dark chocolate into a microwave-safe ziplock bag and microwave until warm and melted. Cut a tiny piece off the corner of the bag (or make a tiny hole with a toothpick) and use to paint your spider web on the icing!

Makes 6-8 servings

THE CURSE OF JAMES DEAN'S CAR

Hollywood idol James Dean was famous for his love of racing as well as for the movies he made. His pride and joy was a silver-gray Porsche Spyder 550, a high-powered German racing car. Studio bosses forbade Dean from racing during the filming of *Giant* in 1955, the movie in which he starred with Elizabeth Taylor and Rock Hudson. The day after filming was completed, the 24-year-old actor jumped in his Porsche and headed north out of Los Angeles for a race that would start the following day. He wouldn't make it to the starting line. A few miles out of the city, Dean crashed into another car at a highway intersection. The oncoming car had paused before finishing a left-hand turn, and the head-on collision killed Dean instantly. The other driver was only slightly injured. From that day forward, bits and pieces of the famous car were sold and caused accidents wherever they went.

The curse first struck a mechanic who was helping unload the battered Porsche from the tow truck. The car slipped and fell on him, breaking both his legs. A doctor who bought the engine and installed it in his

race car, lost control during a race and was killed. In the same race, a car containing the Porsche's driveshaft rolled over and left the driver injured.

Two tires from the car—reported by a mechanic to be in perfect condition—were sold to a race car driver. Both tires exploded simultaneously forcing his car off the road. The state of California put the smashed-up body of Dean's Porsche on exhibition to promote highway safety, but some of those who flocked to the legendary wreck became its innocent victims. While on display in Sacramento, the car broke free of its frame and fell, breaking a teenager's hip. A few weeks later, the phantom car lashed out at the unlucky truck driver who was taking it to its next safety display. The driver had an accident and was thrown from his truck. The Porsche rolled off the back, fell onto the driver who was lying by the road, and killed him. The hand break of another truck, carrying the car in Oregon, suddenly slipped off, which sent the truck crashing into a storefront. In 1959, the crumpled body of the car mysteriously broke into eleven pieces while on display in New Orleans.

Those who dare can visit the monument in Cholame, California, at the intersection where James Dean met his death—and his car took on an evil afterlife.

A Love Spell

Here's a spell that will bring the object of your affection right to your front door.

When the first snowfall of winter comes, build two snowmen in your yard or a nearby park. Make one in your image and the other in the image of the one whose heart you hope to capture. Each snowman must wear something that belongs to the person they represent. Sweeten the spot where the heart of each snowman should be with a little sugar and make sure that they are touching. Then light a votive candle (but do not leave the candle unattended). Recite this charm:

> By this candle that I light
> Let my true love now take flight.
> Lead my love on a magical tour
> Ending outside my front door.

By the time the candle has completely burned out, your beloved will have knocked upon your door.

117

GUESTS

Why are guests so well received at certain houses? The hosts may not be as polite as you think. They could just be superstitious.

Hundreds of years ago, people lived more simply and traveled very little. Communities were fearful of the mysterious world that existed beyond the boundaries of their villages. Witches and ominous gods were thought to live among the surrounding mountains, valleys, and seas. So when a stranger knocked on a family's door, people believed it could be a spirit coming to cast an evil spell on the home. Wanderers were therefore greeted as welcomed guests, and obliged with food and comfort in the hopes they would move on, peaceful and satisfied.

PRANKS

BY ROBERT BLOCH

The lights came on just after sunset.

He stood in the hallway, near the front door, filling the candy dish on the table with a skill born of long practice. How many times had he done this, how many Halloweens had he spent preparing for the joyful hours of the evening ahead? No use trying to remember; he'd lost count. Not that it mattered, really. What mattered was the occasion itself, the few hours of magic and make-believe one was privileged to share with the children. What mattered was the opportunity, however brief, to enter into the spirit of things, participate in the let's-pretend on the one night of the year when a childless couple could themselves pretend that they were truly no different from the members of the community around them; solid, ordinary citizens who took pride in their homes and their offspring.

But truth to tell, it was the make-believe that thrilled him. Maybe they both had a childish streak of their own, dressing up to surprise the youngsters.

Now, hearing her footsteps on the stairs, his eyes brightened in

eager anticipation. One year she'd come sailing down the steps in hoopskirts as Scarlett O'Hara, another time she'd gotten herself up as a black-braided Pocahontas, once she'd worn the powdered wig of a Marie Antoinette. What would he see tonight—Cleopatra, the Empress Josephine, Joan of Arc?

Leave it to her to fathom his expectations and astonish him with the unexpected. And that, as she descended into full view, was exactly what she did. For instead of a figure out of film or fiction he beheld a little old lady with a motherly smile, wearing an apron over a simple housedress, as though she had just stepped out of an old-fashioned country kitchen.

"How do you like it?" she said.

For a moment he stared at her, completely taken aback, yet puzzled by the odd familiarity of her appearance. Where had he seen this smiling elderly woman before? Then, suddenly, his gaze darted toward the candy dish on the table and the empty box beside it. And there on the front of the box was his answer—the oval photographic portrait purporting to represent the candy-maker herself. Tonight she was Mrs. See.

Now it was his turn to smile. "Marvelous!" he said. "It's hard for me to imagine you as an old lady, but I must say you look the part."

She nodded, pleased with his reaction. "I

think the kids will like it. And they certainly should be able to recognize you too, Ben."

He peered at her through the tiny rimless spectacles and patted his paunch. "I hope so. At least I make a better Ben Franklin than last year's Abraham Lincoln. Though I admit I was tempted to try something different for a change. Remember when I did Adolf Hitler—"

"And scared half the children out of their wits?" She shook her head. "Halloween's for fun, not fright. No, I think you made a good choice."

Then the doorbell rang.

She opened the door and the two of them stood side by side, gazing down at the little ragamuffin in the cowboy outfit as he clutched his crumpled shopping bag and rattled off the time-honored greeting. "Trick-or-treat," he said.

She stepped back, smiling. "Isn't he adorable?" she murmured. Then, "Come right in and help yourself. The candy's on the table."

The moment the front door closed, Joe Stuttman turned to Maggie, scowling. "Jesus H. Christ!" he said.

"Now, Joe, please!" Maggie sighed. "Don't get yourself upset over nothing."

"You call that nothing?" His scowl and voice deepened. "Those damned costumes must have cost a

fortune. I'm not blind, you know—I read the ads. Okay, so most of Angela's witch outfit you made yourself, but why in hell you had to go and buy Robbie that fancy space suit—"

"Simmer down," Maggie told him. "You don't have to pay for it. I've been saving up from my household allowance these past two months."

"So that's it!" Joe shook his head. "No wonder we've been eating so many of those lousy casserole messes lately. I work my tail off down at the shop and all I get to eat is glob because your son has to dress up like a goddamn astronaut for Halloween!"

"*Our* son," Maggie said softly. "Robbie's a good boy. You saw his last report card—all those A's mean he's really been doing his homework. And he still finds time to help me around the house and do your yard work for you. I think he deserves a treat once in a while."

"Treat." Joe went over to the coffee table in front of the television set, picked up the six-pack resting there, then yanked out a can of beer. "That's another thing I don't like—this trick-or-treat business. Running up and down the street at night, knocking on doors and asking for a handout. I don't care what kind of a fancy getup a kid's wearing. What's he's really doing is acting like some wino on Main Street, a bum mooching off strangers. You call that good behavior? It's nothing but blackmail if you ask me." He thumbed the beer can tab. "Trick-or-treat—it's a threat, isn't it? Pay up or else. What are you training Robbie for, to grow up and join the Mafia?"

"For heaven's sake," Maggie said, "You don't have to go on a roll

about it. You know as well as I do that trick-or-treat is just a phrase. People expect kids to ask them for candy or cookies on Halloween, it's just a tradition, that's all. And if somebody doesn't come through with a treat I'm sure neither Robbie nor Angela is going to do anything about it. They'll just go on to another house." She glanced unhappily toward the front door. "I only wish you'd let me put out a few little goodies for the kids who come here."

"No way," Joe said. He took a gulp of beer. "I thought we had that all settled. I'm not wasting my money on a mess of junk food for a bunch of little bastards who dress up in stupid costumes and come banging on my front door."

"But, Joe—"

"You heard me." Joe scooped up the six-pack with his free hand. "Now let's get those lights turned off, quick, before anyone shows up. I'm gonna watch the game on the set in the bedroom, and I don't want any interruptions. That means don't answer the door, do you read me?"

"Yes," Maggie said. "I read you."

It seemed to take forever for the twins to get ready; Pam's devil costume was too tight and had to be let out at the waist before it could be zipped up in back, and Debbie kept fussing with her clown makeup.

In point of fact, they didn't actually leave the house until almost eight-fifteen, but within three minutes after their departure Chuck and Linda Cooper were in bed.

"Alone at last!" Linda giggled. "My God, you'd think I was some kind of floozy, sneaking around like this and waiting for a chance to hop into the sack the moment the coast is clear."

"Be a floozy," Chuck said. "Come on, I dare you."

"Don't get me wrong." Linda sobered. "You know how much I love the kids, we both do. But lately it seems like we never get a chance, what with their bedroom right next door to ours and these damned mattress springs squeaking. I'm always afraid they can hear us."

"So let them hear." Chuck grinned. "About time they learned the facts of life."

Linda shook her head. "But they're still so young! Maybe I'm too self-conscious, I don't know. It's the way I was brought up, I guess, and I can't help it."

"Look, let's not talk about it now, shall we?" Chuck tossed the covers aside. "I'm not going to spend the next two hours worrying whether or not the bedsprings squeak."

Sometime around nine-thirty Father Carmichael checked his watch. "Getting late," he said. "I really should be going. I thank you both for a lovely dinner and a delightful evening—"

"Come on, Father, what's your hurry?" Jim Higgins reached for the bottle and leaned forward to pour a good two inches of its contents into the priest's brandy snifter. "One for the road, okay?" he said.

Father Carmichael shrugged in mild protest, but Martha Higgins beamed and nodded at him from her chair beside the fireplace. "Please don't rush away, Billy and Pat should be home soon and I know they'd love to see you."

"I'd like that." The priest twirled his snifter, then raised it to drink, smiling as he did so. Then, as he set the glass down again, his expression changed. "Aren't they a little young to be out at this hour?"

"It's a trick-or-treat night, don't you remember?" Jim Higgins swallowed brandy in a single swig that emptied his own snifter. "After all, Halloween only comes once a year."

"Praise the Lord for that," Father Carmichael said softly.

Martha Higgins raised her eyebrows. "Don't you approve of trick-or-treat?"

"A harmless diversion," the priest told her. "But Halloween itself—"

"Now wait a minute." Jim Higgins spoke quickly, glancing at Martha out of the corner of his eye as he did so. "This is a nice friendly little town. You of all people should know that, Father. I realize a lot of parents go along with their youngsters on a night like this, but we talked it over and decided it was time for Billy and Pat to make the rounds alone if they wanted to. Sort of gives them a grown-up feeling, and helps them to understand there's nothing to be afraid of."

"Nothing to be afraid of." The priest sighed. Then, conscious of Martha Higgins' sudden frown, he forced a smile. "Don't mind me," he

said. "It's the brandy talking."

"What do you mean?" Jim Higgins was frowning too. "What's all this about Halloween? Are you trying to tell us we ought to be afraid of goblins and witches? I thought people stopped believing in that stuff a couple of hundred years ago."

"So they did." Father Carmichael took a hasty sip from his glass. "They stopped believing. But that in itself didn't necessarily stop the phenomena."

"But isn't a lot of that just superstition?" Martha said. "All this nonsense about vampires and werewolves and the dead coming out of their graves? And even if such things were possible, I don't see what it has to do with Halloween. It's just another holiday."

Father Carmichael finished his brandy before speaking. "The real holiday—holy day, that is—will come tomorrow, on the Feast of All Saints. It's then we celebrate Hallowmass in honor of Our Lady and all the martyrs unknown who died to preserve the faith. The faith which Satan abhors, because it affirms the power of Almighty God.

"But Satan too has power. And he chooses to manifest his defiance on the eve of Allhallows by loosing the forces of evil which he commands." The priest broke off, smiling self-consciously. "Forgive me—I didn't mean to start preaching a sermon. And I hope you realize I was just speaking figuratively, so to say."

"Sure thing," Jim Higgins moved to his wife and put his hand on her shoulder. "Just a little Halloween ghost story, right?"

Martha nodded but her eyes were troubled, intent on Father Carmichael as he glanced at his watch again, then rose.

"Time I was leaving," he said. "I take it I'll be seeing you both at Mass tomorrow—"

Martha gestured quickly. "But you haven't seen the children yet! They should be here any minute now. Please, Father. Won't you stay?"

The priest hesitated, conscious that the smile had faded from her face as he stared into the troubled eyes.

"Of course," he said. "Of course I'll stay."

Jim Higgins frowned. "Almost ten-thirty," he murmured. "They promised to be back by ten at the latest." The frown deepened. "You'll pardon my language, Father—but where in hell are those kids?"

"Heavely," Irene Esterhazy said. "I mean heavenly." She lurched against the buffet table as she took another bite of her croissant. "Try one, honey—they're soooo good!"

Howard Esterhazy shook his head. "No time for that," he told her. "We've stayed too long as it is."

Once in the car, with the windows open and the night air fanning her face, Irene sobered slightly. "You mad at me, honey?"

"No." Howard sighed, eyes intent on the road. "I guess you're entitled to a little diversion once in a while. But do you realize what time it is?"

Irene focused her eyes on the illuminated dial of the dashboard

clock. "My God, you're right! It's almost eleven. I had no idea—"

Her husband nodded, "I know. And I didn't want to spoil your fun. It's just that I told Connie we wouldn't be late."

"Maybe we ought to give her a little something extra," Irene said. "She always been so good about sitting with Mark, even though she does play that damn stereo full blast."

"You can say that again," Howard muttered as they pulled up before the house. The wind was rising, sending surges of sound through the treetops, but the screech of the stereo echoed so loudly that even their voices were drowned by its pounding beat as they left the car and moved up to the front door.

But as he fumbled in his pocket the door swung open quickly and Connie peered out, "Oh, it's you—" she said.

"I thought it was Mark." Connie's voice faltered.

"Mark?" Irene moved into the hall, her forehead furrowing. "You mean he isn't here?"

"Turn that thing off," Howard shouted.

Retreating to the living room, Connie hastily obeyed, then turned to confront the Esterhazys' accusing stare.

"Now what's all this about Mark?" Howard said. "Where is he?"

Connie's gaze dropped and her words came with forced bravado. "You know Bill Summers, that friend of his from down the street? Well, he came to the door and I thought it was trick-or-treat, but it turned out he wanted Mark to come out with him. Just around the

block, he said, because he didn't want to go alone. I told Mark no, he wasn't supposed to, and he had all the candy he wanted right here at home that you left for him. Besides, he didn't even have a costume. But Bill said it would only be for a few minutes, and Mark was almost crying, he wanted to go so bad. So I figured why not let him just as long as he promised to come right back and not go off the block? Besides, I told my boyfriend where I was sitting tonight and he called on the phone right in the middle of all this going on, so—"

"Never mind that." Howard's hoarse voice held apprehension as well as anger. "How long ago was this?"

"How long?" Connie shook her head. "I don't know. I mean, I was on the phone and then I started playing the stereo, like maybe around ten o'clock."

"Then he's been gone over an hour." Howard's face was grim. "Maybe an hour and a half, while you sat there blabbing with your boyfriend and listening to that goddamn rock crap!"

Connie began to cry, but Irene ignored her. She turned to her husband. "Why don't you get in the car and take a run around the block? He can't have gone very far."

"I hope to God you're right." Howard moved toward the hall. "Meanwhile, you better phone the Summerses and see if Bill brought him back over there."

"Good idea. I never thought of that." Irene was already dialing as Howard started up the car outside, and she could hear it pulling away as Mrs. Summers responded to her call.

"Hello—Midge?" Irene spoke quickly. "Sorry to bother you at this late hour, but I was wondering—"

Connie stood beside her, trying to control her sniffles as she listened. But Irene's words and the pauses between them told their own story, and when at last she hung up and turned her anguished face to the light Connie started to cry again.

"You heard?" Irene said. "Bill's gone too." Then her voice broke. "Oh my God!" She rose. "What's keeping Howard so long?"

The answer came as a car screeched to a halt in the driveway and Irene opened the front door to admit her husband. The night wind was cold, but what really chilled her as he entered was the realization that Howard was alone.

"No sign of him," he muttered. "I covered everything for a half mile up and down, and there's not a kid out anywhere."

"There wouldn't be, at this hour." Irene nodded. "I know he's not at the Summerses', but maybe he and Bill stopped by somewhere else. I'm going to phone the Coopers and see—"

"Don't bother," Howard said. "I've just come from there. And before that I looked in on the Stuttmans and those new people, Higgins or whatever their name is. Their kids haven't come home either."

"But that's impossible! Do you realize it's past eleven-thirty?"

She trembled, fighting the tears. "Where could they be?"

"We'll find out." Howard brushed past her, striding toward the phone. "I'm calling the police."

The grandfather's clock began to boom its message of midnight as pot-bellied Benjamin Franklin and little old Mrs. See peered into the parlor at the left of the front hallway.

"I'm glad we used candy this time," she said. "And that was a good idea of yours, giving money instead if the youngsters came to the door with their parents."

It was dark in the parlor and they had only a moment to stare through the shadows at the huddled forms lying motionless within.

"How many are there?" he said.

"Thirteen." She beamed at him as the chimes came to an end. "At least we won't be going hungry."

Sergeant Lichner kept his cool, but it wasn't easy. The station was like a madhouse, all those parents yelling and crying, and it took a team of four men just to question them and get some facts, instead of listening to wild guesses about kidnappers or crazies who put razor blades in Halloween candy.

But in the end he got it all together, using the statements to map out a route. Putting through some phone calls to establish where each child or group of children had last been seen, it turned out that everything must have happened somewhere within the area of one square block.

Then he called in backups and started out. There were four black-and-whites assigned to the search, each with its quota of parents, and each taking a single side of the block as they went from door to door asking questions.

On three sides the answers formed a pattern. Various youngsters had knocked on doors at various times, but all had been seen and accounted for.

Sergeant Lichner himself was in a fifth car, and to speed matters up he took one end of the block while the fourth car started at the other.

It wasn't until the two cars converged in the middle of the block to compare notes that he got an answer. Sid Olney pulled up and got out, shaking his head. "They were here, all right," he said. "Stopped at every house back there, right on up until around eleven. What did you find out, anything?"

Sergeant Lichner took a deep breath. "Same as you." He glanced at the house directly behind him. "Folks in the last place said the Esterhazy kid and the Summers boy were there late, almost eleven-thirty. What time did your people see them?"

Sid Olney shook his head. "They didn't." He shook his head. "That's funny."

But there was no mirth in his eyes, or the eyes of the parents as they stared at the spot where the trail ended—the space between the two houses looming on either side of the weed-choked vacant lot lying empty and deserted under the Halloween moon.

How To Counteract Spells

There's nothing worse than being cursed! Here are a few simple ways to counteract a nasty spell, even if you're the one who's been bewitched.

1. Place a penny in your pillowcase, add a piece of birch bark and a sprig of willow. Recite the following charm for a week each night before you go to bed and the curse will disappear:

   A lucky penny in my pillow,
   A piece of birch bark and some willow.
   I give these gifts to you my friend,
   So that this curse on me may end.

2. With adult supervision, take a wax figure of the witch or wizard who cast the spell and melt it in a pot. Dig a hole in the dirt at least two feet deep and pour in the hot wax. Bury it there and cover the fresh earth with mint and sage.

3. If you are fortunate enough to be there when the curse is cast upon you, extend one arm, spread all five fingers in front of your enemy's face and shout, "REVERSE THE CURSE!" The spell will bounce right off your hand and back onto the one who performed it.

The Salem Witch Trials

It all began in the village of Salem, Massachusetts in January of 1692 when two girls, Elizabeth Parris and Abigail Williams, began to show unusual symptoms: screaming, convulsions, and trance-like behavior. The doctor declared that their fits could mean only one thing: the girls were under the influence of witches.

Soon many girls throughout Salem Village were complaining of similar symptoms. They jumped into holes, crept under chairs, and contorted their bodies in all sorts of ways. Others, especially in the company of one particular minister, made strange sounds and pulled burning logs from fireplaces, throwing them about the room. Though the people prayed and fasted, the fits continued. Fingers were pointed first to the weakest and strangest of the village: Tituba, a slave from Barbados; Sarah Good, a beggar; and Sarah Osborne, an old bedridden woman.

But as the panic grew, more and more people once deemed "respectable" were also accused, including Goodwife Proctor, whose husband was a successful farmer and tavern keeper; Martha Cory, the wife of a farmer and landowner; the governor's wife; and even a four-year-old girl by the name of Dorcas Good.

A special court was established in Salem to hear the cases and the trials began in June. Bridget Bishop was the first to be tried and hanged. But the case that drew the most attention was Rebecca Nurse's, a 71-year-old church member and the most saint-like little old lady of the village. It was her trial that started to cast a shadow of doubt over the witch hunting. The jury acquitted her at first, but the judge finally found her guilty and she also was put to the gallows.

By October, the governor ordered the special court disbanded and the trials came to an end. Those awaiting trial or execution were released and pardoned. Little Dorcas Good and Tituba were freed, but Sarah Good and Sarah Osborne both died in the gallows.

Hundreds were accused and 150 imprisoned and chained to prison walls. In all, 20 people were hanged and many more perished in prison.

THE VIPER

ANONYMOUS

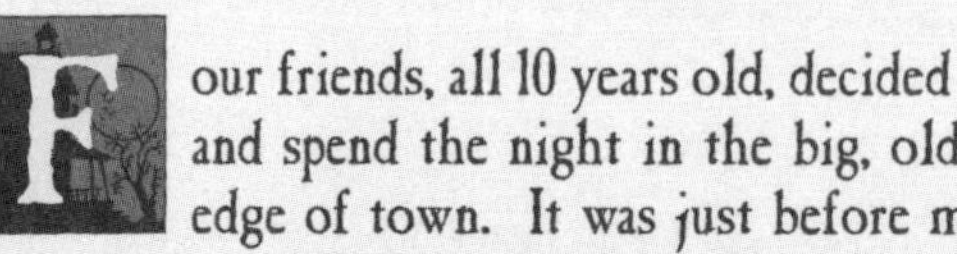

Four friends, all 10 years old, decided to challenge their fears and spend the night in the big, old haunted house on the edge of town. It was just before midnight and they were down in the candle lit, cobweb filled, dusky cellar scaring each other with ghost stories when there was a loud banging on the window and a low, croaking voice called out, "I am the Viper!"

The boys, in unison, screamed and high tailed it up the creaky stairs to the entry hall. They stood there panting and shaking when all of a sudden there was a dull thudding at the front door and the same soulless voice groaned, "I am the Viper!" Not knowing where else to go, the boys scrambled up the wide stairs to the next story and stood huddled on the landing, ashen faced, their knees rattling.

It was quiet for a long time and they began to slowly relax when, without warning, the big window, not three feet in front of them, began to rattle violently. From the other side the voice, louder, impatient bellowed, "I am the Viper!" The boys, eyes bulging and dry, hollow gurgles coming from their throats, flew up the stairs to the next floor, which was the attic. Because of the low roof they were forced to sit in the middle of the floor, holding on to each other for dear life.

Intermittent sobs and snuffles broke the stony silence. The boys could hear the sounds of rats scurrying about in the darkness and the flapping of bat wings as they flew out of a hole in the roof. Time seemed to stand still as the boys contemplated a gruesome death at the hands of this diabolical creature.

Then they heard it. It started as a low, deep rumbling, like thunder in the distance. The voice quickly grew louder, building in crescendo, until the entire house shook and seemed engulfed in the violent reverberations. "I AM THE VIPER!" The shutters in front of them blasted open, snapping from their hinges, and a hairy, haggard, misshapen face peered in through the opening. Green eyes glowed in the dark from the center of that horrible face. Bloodless lips parted, revealing a toothless, black opening. "I AM THE VIPER!" And then, with a twinkle in his eyes and a slight smile on his face, he muttered, "I come to vipe your vindows!"

Vampires first appeared in Slavic folktales about 1000 years ago. Plagued by disease and death—which were completely mysterious in those days—villagers blamed "corpses that traveled at night and sucked the blood from victims." This explanation for the troubles and, more importantly, being able to take a course of action against them, relieved anxiety in the community. Thus peasants eager to rid the village of this malevolence often dug up graves and dispatched those with signs of being a vampire by impaling the heart with a steak or beheading it. Furthermore, to keep the undead out of the house, garlic, religious symbols or exposure to daylight were thought to work.

Over the years vampires acquired various characteristics such as superhuman strength and speed, hypnotic mind control and inhuman stealth. As for looks, Bram Stoker's Dracula was a tall, older man with a long white moustache, pale, pointy ears and hairs in the center of his palms, while tuxedoed Bela Lugosi was a suave aristocrat. But the vampire's ability to shape-shift (mostly into bats or mist), is nowhere more stunning than its metamorphosis from, bloated, undead villagers to Tom Cruise and Brad Pitt.

GINGERBREAD GHOSTS

Better gobble these cookies down quick—they've been known to disappear!

Cookies
2/3 cup shortening
3/4 cup sifted light brown sugar
2 tablespoons molasses
3 tablespoons boiled, then cooled water
2 teaspoon grated lemon rind
2 1/4 cups sifted all-purpose flour
1 teaspoon baking soda
1 teaspoon cinnamon
1 1/2 teaspoons cloves
1 teaspoon ground cardamom seeds

1. Preheat oven to 350°F. Grease a cookie sheet.
2. In a large bowl, cream together shortening and sugar. Add molasses, water and lemon rind.
3. In a seperate bowl, combine flour, baking soda, cinnamon, cloves and cardamom and add gradually to the creamed mixture. Mix well.
4. Toss dough on a floured surface. Shape into loaf and chill for at least 30 minutes.
5. Remove chilled dough and place on floured surface. Roll out dough very thin.
6. Using ghost shaped cookie cutters, cut out cookies from dough and place on cookie sheet. Bake 8-10 minutes.
7. Allow cookies to cool before icing.

Icing
3 egg whites
1 pound confectioners' sugar
1 tablespoon white vinegar

1. In a bowl, beat egg whites lightly with a fork.
2. Add sugar and beat with an electric mixer on lowest speed for 1 minute.
3. Add vinegar and beat on high speed for 2 more minutes, or until stiff and glossy.
4. Use a pastry tube to decorate with icing.

Makes about 60 cookies

THE JUDGE'S HOUSE

BY BRAM STOKER

When the time for his examination drew near, Malcolm Malcolmson made up his mind to go somewhere to read by himself. He packed a portmanteau with some clothes and all the books he required, and then took ticket for the first name on the local timetable which he did not know.

When at the end of three hours' journey he alighted at Benchurch, he felt satisfied that he had so far obliterated his tracks as to be sure of having a peaceful opportunity of pursuing his studies. He went straight to the one inn which the sleepy little place contained, and put up for the night. Malcolmson looked around the day after his arrival to try to find quarters more isolated than even so quiet an inn as "The good Traveller" afforded. There was only one place which took his fancy, and it certainly satisfied his wildest ideas regarding quiet; in fact, quiet was not the proper word to apply to it—desolation was the only term conveying any suitable idea of its isolation. It was an old rambling, heavy-built house of the Jacobean style, with heavy gables and windows, unusually small, and set higher than was customary in such houses, and was surrounded with a high brick wall, massively built. Indeed, on examination, it looked more like a fortified

house than an ordinary dwelling. But all these things pleased Malcolmson. His joy was increased when he realized beyond doubt that it was not at present inhabited.

From the post office he got the name of the agent, who was rarely surprised at the application to rent a part of the old house. Mr. Carnford, the local lawyer and agent, was a genial old gentleman, and frankly confessed his delight at anyone being willing to live in the house. "To tell you the truth," said he, "I should be only too happy, on behalf of the owners, to let anyone have the house rent free for a term of years if only to accustom the people here to see it inhabited. It has been so long empty that some kind of absurd prejudice has grown up about it, and this can be best put down by its occupation—if only," he added with a sly glance at Malcolmson, "by a scholar like yourself, who wants it quiet for a time."

Malcolmson thought it needless to ask the agent about the "absurd prejudice"; he knew he would get more information, if he should require it, on that subject from other quarters. He paid his three months' rent, got a receipt, and the name of an old woman who would probably undertake to "do" for him, and came away with the keys in his pocket. He then went to the landlady of the inn, who was a cheerful and most kindly person, and asked her advice as to such stores and provisions as he would be likely to require. She threw up her hands in amazement when he told her where he was going to settle

himself.

"Not in the Judge's House!" she said, and grew pale as she spoke. He explained the locality of the house, saying that he did not know its name.

When he had finished she answered, "It is the Judge's House sure enough." He asked her to tell him about the place. She told him that it was so called locally because it had been many years before—how long she could not say, as she was herself from another part of the country, but she thought it must have been a hundred years or more—the abode of a judge who was held in great terror on account of his harsh sentences and his hostility to prisoners at Assizes. As to what there was against the house itself she could not tell. She had often asked, but no one could inform her; but there was a general feeling that there was *something*, and for her own part she would not take all the money in Drinkwater's Bank and stay in the house an hour by herself. Then she apologized to Malcolmson for her disturbing talk.

"It is too bad of me, sir, and you—and a young gentleman, too—if you will pardon me saying it, going to live there all alone. If you were my boy you wouldn't sleep there a night, not if I had to go there myself and pull the big alarm bell that's on the roof!" The good creature was so manifestly in earnest, and was so kindly in her intentions, that Malcolmson, although amused, was touched.

He told her kindly how much he appreciated her interest in him, and added, "But, my dear Mrs. Witham, indeed you need not be

concerned about me! A man who is reading for the Mathematical Tripos has too much to think of to be disturbed by any of these mysterious 'somethings,' and his work is of too exact and prosaic a kind to allow of his having any corner in his mind for mysteries of any kind. Harmonical Progression, Permutations and Combinations, and Elliptic Functions have sufficient mysteries for me!" Mrs. Witham kindly undertook to see after his commissions, and he went himself to look for the old woman who had been recommended to him.

When he returned to the Judge's House with her, after an interval of a couple of hours, he found Mrs. Witham herself waiting with several men and boys carrying parcels, and an upholsterer's man with a bed in a cart. She was evidently curious to see the inside of the house; and though manifestly so afraid of the "somethings" that at the slightest sound she clutched on to Malcolmson, whom she never left for a moment, went over the whole place.

After his examination of the house, Malcolmson decided to take up his abode in the great dining room; and Mrs. Witham, with the aid of the charwoman, Mrs. Dempster, proceeded to arrange matters. When the hampers were brought in and unpacked, Malcolmson saw that with much kind forethought she had sent from her own kitchen sufficient provisions to last for a few days. Before going she expressed all sorts of kind wishes; and at the door turned and said, "And perhaps, sir, as the room is big and draughty it might be well to have one of those big screens

put round your bed at night—though, truth to tell, I would die myself if I were to be so shut in with all kinds of—of 'things,' that put their heads round the sides, or over the top, and look on me!" The image which she had called up was too much for her nerves, and she fled incontinently.

Mrs. Dempster sniffed in a superior manner as the landlady disappeared, and remarked that for her own part she wasn't afraid of all the bogies in the kingdom. "I'll tell you what it is, sir," she said, "bogies is all kinds and sorts of things—except bogies! Rats and mice, and beetles; and creaky doors, and loose slates, and broken panes. Look at the wainscot of the room! It is old—hundreds of years old! Do you think there's no rats and beetles there! And do you imagine, sir, that you won't see none of them! Rats is bogies, I tell you, and bogies is rats; and don't you get to think anything else!" She set to work with her cleaning; and by nightfall, when Malcolmson returned from his walk he found the room swept and tidied, a fire burning in the old hearth, the lamp lit, and the table spread for supper with Mrs. Witham's excellent fare. "This is comfort, indeed," he said, as he rubbed his hands.

When he had finished his supper, he got out his books again, put fresh wood on the fire, trimmed his lamp, and set himself down to a spell of real hard work. He went on without a pause till about eleven o'clock, when he knocked off for a bit to fix his fire and lamp, and to make himself a cup of tea. He had always been a tea drinker, and during his college life had sat late at work and had taken tea late. The rest

was a great luxury to him, and he enjoyed it with a sense of delicious, voluptuous ease. As he sipped his hot tea he revelled in the sense of isolation from his kind. Then it was that he began to notice for the first time what a noise the rats were making.

"Surely," he thought, "they cannot have been at it all the time I was reading. Had they been, I must have noticed it!" Presently, when the noise increased, he satisfied himself that it was really new. It was evident that at first the rats had been frightened at the presence of a stranger, and the light of fire and lamp; but that as the time went on they had grown bolder and were now disporting themselves as was their wont.

How busy they were! and hark to the strange noises! Up and down behind the old wainscot, over the ceiling and under the floor they raced, and gnawed, and scratched! Malcolmson smiled to himself as he recalled to mind the saying of Mrs. Dempster, "Bogies is rats, and rats is bogies!" The tea began to have its effect of intellectual and nervous stimulus; he saw with joy another long spell of work to be done before the night was past, and in the sense of security which it gave him, he allowed himself the luxury of a good look round the room. He took his lamp in one hand, and went all around, wondering that so quaint and beautiful an old house had been so long neglected. There were some old pictures on the walls, but they were coated so thick with dust and dirt that he could not distin-

guish any detail of them, though he held his lamp as high as he could over his head. Here and there as he went round, he saw some crack or hole blocked for a moment by the face of a rat with its bright eyes glittering in the light, but in an instant it was gone, and a squeak and a scamper followed.

The thing that most struck him, however, was the rope of the great alarm bell on the roof, which hung down in a corner of the room on the right-hand side of the fireplace. He pulled up close to the hearth a great high-backed carved oak chair, and sat down to his last cup of tea. When this was done he made up the fire, and went back to his work sitting at the corner of the table, having the fire to his left. For a while the rats disturbed him somewhat with their perpetual scampering, but he got accustomed to the noise, and he became so immersed in his work that everything in the world, except the problem which he was trying to solve, passed away from him.

He suddenly looked up, his problem was still unsolved, and there was in the air that sense of the hour before dawn, which is so dread to doubtful life. The noise of the rats had ceased. Indeed it seemed to him that it must have ceased but lately and that it was the sudden cessation which had disturbed him. As he looked, he started in spite of his *sang froid*.

There on the great high-backed carved oak chair by the right side of the fireplace sat an enormous rat, steadily glaring at him with baleful eyes. He made a motion to it as though to hunt it away, but it

did not stir. Then he made the motion of throwing something. Still it did not stir, but showed its great white teeth angrily, and its cruel eyes shone in the lamplight with an added vindictiveness.

Malcolmson felt amazed, and seizing the poker from the hearth ran at it to kill it. Before, however, he could strike it, the rat, with a squeak that sounded like the concentration of hate, jumped upon the floor, and, running up the rope of the alarm bell, disappeared in the darkness. Instantly, strange to say, the noisy scampering of the rats in the wainscot began again.

By this time Malcolmson's mind was quite off the problem; and as a shrill cock-crow outside told him of the approach of morning, he went to bed and to sleep.

He slept so sound that he was not even waked by Mrs. Dempster coming in to make up his room. It was only when she had tidied up the place and got his breakfast ready and tapped on the screen which closed in his bed that he woke. He was a little tired still after his night's hard work, but a strong cup of tea soon freshened him up, and, taking his book, he went out for his morning walk. On his return he looked in to see Mrs. Witham and to thank her for her kindness. When she saw him coming through the bay window of her sanctum, she came out to meet him and asked him in.

She looked at him searchingly and shook her head as she said, "You must not overdo it, sir. You are paler this morning than you should be. Too late hours and too hard work on the brain isn't good for

any man! But tell me, sir, how did you pass the night? But, my heart! sir, I was glad when Mrs. Dempster told me this morning that you were all right and sleeping sound when she went in."

"Oh, I was all right," he answered, smiling, "the 'somethings' didn't worry me, as yet. Only the rats; and they had a circus, I tell you, all over the place. There was one wicked looking old devil that sat up on my own chair by the fire, and wouldn't go till I took the poker to him, and then he ran up the rope of the alarm bell and got to somewhere up the wall or the ceiling—I couldn't see where, it was so dark."

"Mercy on us," said Mrs. Witham, "an old devil, and sitting on a chair by the fireside! Take care, sir! take care! There's many a true word spoken in jest."

"How do you mean? 'Pon my word I don't understand."

"An old devil! The old devil, perhaps. There! sir, you needn't laugh," for Malcolmson had broken into a hearty peal. "You young folks thinks it easy to laugh at things that makes older ones shudder. Never mind, sir! never mind! Please God, you'll laugh all the time. It's what I wish you myself!" and the good lady beamed all over in sympathy with his enjoyment, her fears gone for a moment.

"Oh, forgive me!" said Malcolmson presently. "Don't think me rude; but the idea was too much for me—that the old devil himself was on the chair last night!" And at the thought he laughed again. Then he went home to dinner.

This evening the scampering of the rats began earlier; indeed it

had been going on before his arrival, and only ceased whilst his presence, by its freshness, disturbed them. After dinner he began to work as before. Tonight the rats disturbed him more than they had done on the previous night. Now and again as they disturbed him Malcolmson made a sound to frighten them, smiting the table with his hand or giving a fierce "Hsh, hsh," so that they fled straightway to their holes.

And so the early part of the night wore on; and despite the noise Malcolmson got more and more immersed in his work.

All at once he stopped, as on the previous night, being overcome by a sudden sense of silence. There was not the faintest sound of gnaw, or scratch, or squeak. The silence was as of the grave. He remembered the odd occurrence of the previous night, and instinctively he looked at the chair standing close by the fireside. And then a very odd sensation thrilled through him.

There, on the great old high-backed carved oak chair beside the fireplace sat the same enormous rat, steadily glaring at him with baleful eyes.

Instinctively he took the nearest thing to his hand, a book of logarithms, and flung it at it. The book was badly aimed and the rat did not stir, so again the poker performance of the previous night was repeated; and again the rat, being closely pursued, fled up the rope of the alarm bell.

Strangely too, the departure of this rat was instantly followed by the renewal of the noise made by the general rat community. On

this occasion, as on the previous one, Malcolmson could not see at what part of the room the rat disappeared, for the green shade of his lamp left the upper part of the room in darkness, and the fire had burned low.

On looking at his watch he found it was close on midnight; and he made up his fire and made himself his nightly pot of tea. He had got through a good spell of work, and thought himself entitled to a cigarette; so he sat on the great carved oak chair before the fire and enjoyed it. Whilst smoking he began to think that he would like to know where the rat disappeared to, for he had certain ideas for the morrow not entirely disconnected with a rat trap. Accordingly he lit another lamp and placed it so that it would shine well into the right-hand corner of the wall by the fireplace. Then he got all the books he had with him, and placed them handy to throw at the vermin. Finally he lifted the rope of the alarm bell and placed the end of it on the table, fixing the extreme end under the lamp. As he handled it he could not help noticing how pliable it was, especially for so strong a rope, and one not in use. "You could hang a man with it," he thought to himself.

When his preparations were made he looked around, and said complacently, "There now, my friend, I think we shall learn something of you this time!" He began his work again, and though as before somewhat disturbed at first by the noise of the rats, soon lost himself in his propositions and problems.

Again he was called to his immediate surroundings suddenly. This time it might not have been the sudden silence only which took his attention; there was a slight movement of the rope, and the lamp moved. Without stirring, he looked to see if his pile of books was within range, and then cast his eye along the rope. As he looked he saw the great rat drop from the rope on the oak armchair and sit there glaring at him. He raised a book in his right hand, and taking careful aim, flung it at the rat. The latter, with a quick movement, sprang aside and dodged the missile. He then took another book, and a third, and flung them one after another at the rat, but each time unsuccessfully. At last, as he stood with a book poised in his hand to throw, the rat squeaked and seemed to be afraid. This made Malcolmson more than ever eager to strike, and the book flew and struck the rat a resounding blow. It gave a terrified squeak, and turning on its pursuer a look of terrible malevolence, ran up the chairback and made a great jump to the rope of the alarm bell and ran up it like lightning. The lamp rocked under the sudden strain, but it was a heavy one and did not topple over. Malcolmson kept his eyes on the rat, and saw it by the light of the second lamp leap to a molding of the wainscot and disappear through a hole in one of the great pictures which hung on the wall, obscured and invisible through its coating of dirt and dust.

"I shall look up my friend's habitation in the morning," said the student, as he went over to collect his books. "The third picture from the fireplace; I shall not forget." He picked up the books one by one,

commenting on them as he lifted them. "*Conic Sections* he does not mind, nor *Cycloidal Oscillations*, nor the *Principia*, nor *Quaternions*, nor *Thermodynamics*. Now for the book that fetched him!"

Malcolmson took it up and looked at it. As he did so he started, and a sudden pallor overspread his face. He looked round uneasily and shivered slightly, as he murmured to himself, "The Bible my mother gave me! What an odd coincidence." He sat down to work again, and the rats in the wainscot renewed their gambols. They did not disturb him, however; somehow their presence gave him a sense of companionship. But he could not attend to his work, and after striving to master the subject on which he was engaged, gave it up in despair, and went to bed as the first streak of dawn stole in through the eastern window.

He slept heavily but uneasily, and dreamed much; and when Mrs. Dempster woke him late in the morning he seemed ill at ease, and for a few minutes did not seem to realize exactly where he was. His first request rather surprised the servant.

"Mrs. Dempster, when I am out today, I wish you would get the steps and dust or wash those pictures—specially that one, the third from the fireplace—I want to see what they are."

Late in the afternoon Malcolmson worked at his books in the shaded walk, and the cheerfulness of the previous day came back to him as the day wore on, and he found that his reading was progressing well. He had worked out to a satisfactory conclusion all the problems which had as yet baffled him, and it was in a state of jubilation that he

paid a visit to Mrs. Witham at "The Good Traveler." He found a stranger in the cozy sitting-room with the landlady, who was introduced to him as Dr. Thornhill. She was not quite at ease, and this, combined with the Doctor's plunging at once into a series of questions, made Malcolmson come to the conclusion that his presence was not an accident. So without preliminary he said, "Dr. Thornhill, I shall with pleasure answer you any question you may choose to ask me if you will answer me one question first."

The Doctor seemed surprised, but he smiled and answered at once. "Done! What is it?"

"Did Mrs. Witham ask you to come here and advise me?"

Dr. Thornhill for a moment was taken aback, and Mrs. Witham got fiery red and turned away; but the Doctor was a frank and ready man, and he answered at once and openly. "She did, but she didn't intend you to know it. She told me that she did not like the idea of your being in that house all by yourself, and that she thought you took too much strong tea. In fact, she wants me to advise you, if possible, to give up the tea and the very late hours. I was a keen student in my time, so I suppose I may take the liberty of a college man, and without offense, advise you not quite as a stranger."

Malcolmson with a smile held out his hand. "Shake! as they say in America," he said. "I must thank you for your kindness and Mrs. Witham too, and your kindness deserves a return on my part. I promise to take no more strong tea—no tea at all till you let me—and I shall go to bed tonight at one o'clock at latest. Will that do?"

"Capital," said the Doctor. "Now tell us all that you noticed in the old house," and so Malcolmson, then and there, told in minute detail all that had happened in the last two nights. He was interrupted every now and then by some exclamation from Mrs. Witham, till finally when he told of the episode of the Bible the landlady's pent-up emotions found vent in a shriek; and it was not till a stiff glass of brandy and water had been administered that she grew composed again.

Dr. Thornhill listened with a face of growing gravity, and when the narrative was complete and Mrs. Witham had been restored he asked, "The rat always went up the rope of the alarm bell?"

"Always."

"I suppose you know," said the Doctor after a pause, "what the rope is?"

"No!"

"It is," said the Doctor slowly, "the very rope which the hangman used for all the victims of the Judge's judicial rancor!" Here he was interrupted by another scream from Mrs. Witham, and steps had to be taken for her recovery. Malcolmson having looked at his watch, and found that it was close to his dinner hour, had gone home before her complete recovery.

When Mrs. Witham was herself again she almost assailed the Doctor with angry questions as to what he meant by putting such horrible ideas into the poor man's mind.

Dr. Thornhill replied, "My dear madam, I had a distinct purpose

in it! I wanted to draw his attention to the bell rope, and to fix it there. It may be that he is in a highly overwrought state, and has been studying too much, although I am bound to say that he seems as sound and healthy a young man, mentally and bodily, as ever I saw—but then the rats—and that suggestion of the devil." The doctor shook his head and went on. "I would have offered to go and stay the first night with him but that I felt sure it would have been a cause of offense. He may get in the night some strange fright or hallucination; and if he does, I want him to pull that rope. All alone as he is it will give us warning, and we may reach him in time to be of service. Do not be alarmed if Benchurch gets a surprise before morning."

"Oh, Doctor, what do you mean? What do you mean?"

"I mean this; that possibly—nay, more probably—we shall hear the great alarm bell from the Judge's House tonight," and the Doctor made about as effective an exit as could be thought of.

When Malcolmson arrived home he found that it was a little after his usual time, and Mrs. Dempster had gone away. For a few minutes after his entrance the noise of the rats ceased; but so soon as they became accustomed to his presence they began again. He was glad to hear them, for he felt once more the feeling of companionship in their noise, and his mind ran back to the strange fact that they only ceased

to manifest themselves when that other—the great rat with the baleful eyes—came upon the scene. The reading lamp only was lit, and its green shade kept the ceiling and the upper part of the room in darkness, so that the cheerful light from the hearth, spreading over the floor and shining on the white cloth laid over the end of the table, was warm and cheery. Malcolmson sat down to his dinner with a good appetite and a buoyant spirit. After his dinner and a cigarette he sat steadily down to work, determined not to let anything disturb him.

For an hour or so he worked all right, and then his thoughts began to wander from his books. The actual circumstances around him, the calls on his physical attention, and his nervous susceptibility were not to be denied. By this time the wind had become a gale, and the gale a storm. Even the great alarm bell on the roof must have felt the force of the wind, for the rope rose and fell slightly, as though the bell were moved a little from time to time, and the limber rope fell on the oak floor with a hard and hollow sound.

As Malcolmson listened to it he bethought himself of the doctor's words, "It is the rope which the hangman used for the victims of the Judge's judicial rancour," and he went over to the corner of the fireplace and took it in his hand to look at it. There seemed a sort of deadly interest in it, and as he stood there he lost himself for a moment in speculation as to who these victims were, and the grim wish of the Judge to have such a ghastly relic ever under his eyes. As he stood there the swaying of the bell on the roof still lifted the

rope now and again; but presently there came a new sensation—a sort of tremor in the rope, as though something was moving along it.

Looking up instinctively Malcolmson saw the great rat coming slowly down towards him, glaring at him steadily. He dropped the rope and started back with a muttered curse, and the rat turning ran up the rope again and disappeared, and at the same instant, Malcolmson became conscious that the noise of the rats, which had ceased for a while, began again.

All this set him thinking, and it occurred to him that he had not investigated the lair of the rat or looked at the pictures, as he had intended. He lit the other lamp, and, holding it up, went and stood opposite the third picture from the fireplace on the right-hand side where he had seen the rat disappear on the previous night.

At the first glance he started back so suddenly that he almost dropped the lamp, and a deadly pallor overspread his face. But he was young and plucky, and pulled himself together, and after the pause of a few seconds stepped forward again, raised the lamp, and examined the picture which had been dusted and washed, and now stood out clearly.

It was of a judge dressed in his robes of scarlet and ermine. His face was strong and merciless, evil, crafty, and vindictive, with a sensual mouth, hooked nose of ruddy colour, and shaped like the beak of a bird of prey. The eyes were of peculiar brilliance and with a terribly malignant expression. As he looked at them, Malcolmson grew cold, for he saw there the very counterpart of the eyes of the great rat. The

lamp almost fell from his hand, he saw the rat with its baleful eyes peering out through the hole in the corner of the picture, and noted the sudden cessation of the noise of the other rats. However, he pulled himself together, and went on with his examination of the picture.

The Judge was seated in a great high-backed carved oak chair, on the right-hand side of a great stone fireplace where, in the corner, a rope hung down from the ceiling, its end lying coiled on the floor. With a feeling of something like horror, Malcolmson recognized the scene of the room as it stood, and gazed around in an awe struck manner as though he expected to find some strange presence behind him. Then he looked over to the corner of the fireplace—and with a loud cry he let the lamp fall from his hand.

There, in the Judge's armchair, with the rope hanging behind, sat the rat with the Judge's baleful eyes, now intensified and with a fiendish leer. Save for the howling of the storm without there was silence.

The fallen lamp recalled Malcolmson to himself. Fortunately it was of metal, and so the oil was not spilt. However, the practical need of attending to it settled at once his nervous apprehensions. When he had turned it out, he wiped his brow and thought for a moment.

"This will not do," he said to himself. "If I go on like this I shall become a crazy fool. This must stop! I promised the Doctor I would not take tea. Faith, he was pretty right! My nerves must have been getting into a queer state. Funny I did not notice it. I never felt better in my life. However, it is all right now, and I shall not be such a fool again." Then he mixed himself a good stiff glass of brandy and water

and resolutely sat down to his work.

It was nearly an hour when he looked up from his book, disturbed by the sudden stillness. Malcolmson listened attentively, and presently heard a thin, squeaking noise, very faint. It came from the corner of the room where the rope hung down, and he thought it was the creaking of the rope on the floor as the swaying of the bell raised and lowered it. Looking up, however, he saw in the dim light the great rat clinging to the rope and gnawing it. The rope was already nearly gnawed through—he could see the lighter colour where the strands were laid bare. As he looked the job was completed, and the severed end of the rope fell clattering on the oaken floor, whilst for an instant the great rat remained like a knob or tassel at the end of the rope, which now began to sway to and fro. Malcolmson felt for a moment another pang of terror as he thought that now the possibility of calling the outer world to his assistance was cut off, but an intense anger took its place, and seizing the book he was reading he hurled it at the rat. The blow was well aimed, but before the missile could reach it the rat dropped off and struck the floor with a soft thud. Malcolmson instantly rushed over towards it, but it darted away and disappeared in the darkness of the shadows of the room. Malcolmson felt that his work was over for the night, and determined then and there to vary the monotony of the proceedings by a hunt for the rat. From where he stood, Malcolmson saw right opposite to him the third picture on the wall from the right of the fireplace. He rubbed his eyes in surprise, and

then a great fear began to come upon him.

In the center of the picture was a great irregular patch of brown canvas, as fresh as when it was stretched on the frame. The background was as before, with chair and chimney-corner and rope, but the figure of the Judge had disappeared.

Malcolmson, almost in a chill of horror, turned slowly round, and then he began to shake and tremble like a man in a palsy. His strength seemed to have left him, and he was incapable of action or movement, hardly even of thought. He could only see and hear.

There, on the great high-backed carved oak chair sat the Judge in his robes of scarlet and ermine, with his baleful eyes glaring vindictively, and a smile of triumph on the resolute, cruel mouth, as he lifted with his hands a *black cap.* Malcolmson felt as if the blood was running from his heart, as one does in moments of prolonged suspense. There was a singing in his ears. Without, he could hear the roar and howl of the tempest, and through it, swept on the storm, came the striking of midnight by the great chimes in the marketplace. He stood for a space of time that seemed to him endless, still as a statue and with wide-open, horror-struck eyes, breathless. As the clock struck, so the smile of triumph on the Judge's face intensified, and at the last stroke of midnight he placed the black cap on his head.

Slowly and deliberately the Judge rose from his chair and picked up the piece of rope of the alarm bell which lay on the floor, drew it through his hands as if he enjoyed the touch, and then deliber-

ately began to know one end of it, fashioning it into a noose. Then he began to move along the table on the opposite side to Malcolmson, keeping his eyes on him until he had passed him, when with a quick movement he stood in front of the door. Malcolmson then began to feel that he was trapped, and tried to think of what he should do. There was some fascination in the Judge's eyes, which he never took off him, and he had, perforce, to look. He saw the Judge approach—still keeping between him and the door—and raise the noose and throw it towards him as if to entangle him. With a great effort he made a quick movement to one side, and saw the rope fall beside him, and heard it strike the oaken floor. Again the Judge raised the noose and tried to ensnare him, ever keeping his baleful eyes fixed on him, and each time by a mighty effort the student just managed to evade it. So this went on for many times, the Judge seeming never discouraged nor discomposed at failure, but playing as a cat does with a mouse. At last, in despair which had reached its climax, Malcolmson cast a quick glance round him. The lamp seemed to have blazed up, and there was a fairly good light in the room. At the many rat-holes and in the chinks and crannies of the wainscot he saw the rats' eyes; and this aspect, that was purely physical, gave him a gleam of comfort. He looked around and saw that the rope of the great alarm bell was laden with rats. Every inch of it was covered with them, and more and more were pouring through the small circular hole in the ceiling whence it emerged, so that with their weight the bell was beginning to sway. Hark! it had swayed till

the clapper had touched the bell. The sound was but a tiny one, but the bell was only beginning to sway, and it would increase.

At the sound the Judge, who had been keeping his eyes fixed on Malcolmson, looked up, and a scowl of diabolical anger overspread his face. A dreadful peal of thunder broke overhead as he raised the rope again, whilst the rats kept running up and down the rope as though working against time. This time, instead of throwing it, he drew close to his victim, and held open the noose as he approached. As he came closer there seemed something paralyzing in his very presence, and Malcolmson stood rigid as a corpse. He felt the Judge's icy fingers touch his throat as he adjusted the rope. Then the Judge, taking the rigid form of the student in his arms, carried him over and placed him standing in the oak chair, and stepping up beside him, put his hand up and caught the end of the swaying rope of the alarm bell. As he raised his hand the rats fled squeaking, and disappeared through the hole in the ceiling. Taking the end of the noose which was round Malcolmson's neck he tied it to the hanging bell-rope, and then descending, pulled away the chair.

When the alarm bell of the Judge's House began to sound a crowd soon assembled. They knocked loudly at the door, but there was no reply. Then they burst in the door, and poured into the great dining room, the Doctor at the head. There at the end of the rope of the great alarm bell hung the body of the student, and on the face of the Judge in the picture was a malignant smile.

Houdini

The great Harry Houdini! We've all heard of this amazing magician and master escape artist. But who was the man behind the spectacle?

Harry Houdini was not born a great magician. In fact, he wasn't even born Harry Houdini! His real name was Ehrich Weiss. The son of two poor Hungarian immigrants, he adopted the name Houdini when, as a seventeen-year-old boy, he read the memoirs of Robert Houdin, a famous master of deception. Inspired by Houdin's story, Ehrich spontaneously committed himself to a life of illusion, and changed his name to Harry Houdini.

Like many magicians, the young Houdini started out with complicated card tricks. But it wasn't long before he discovered his talent for escaping handcuffs and other complex restraints. Although no one knows how Houdini accomplished such feats, his slight build and small hands certainly contributed to his unusual abilities. His claim that there was no restraint from which he could not escape intrigued and excited the public. Before long he had wowed American audiences with his sensational escapes from prisons, straightjackets, and handcuffs. But his greatest feats still lay ahead. . .

In 1900, Houdini sailed for Europe. London was considered to be heart of the performing arts and Houdini was determined to make his name there. He wasted little time beginning his meteoric rise to fame. One of his most notorious public escapes occurred in 1904. A British newspaper challenged Houdini to escape a specially designed pair of cuffs with six sets of locks. He succeeded in just over an hour, astounding more than four thousand spectators who had gathered to watch. Houdini traveled throughout Europe accepting any escape challenge no matter how complicated or death-defying. Whether suspended in mid-air, thrown off a bridge, or submerged underwater, Houdini successfully executed his dangerous escapes every time. During the following years he would release himself from sealed crates, shackles and chains, locked water cans—even the carcass of an enormous sea monster!

By the time of his death in 1926, the miraculous Harry Houdini had become the most famous entertainer of his kind. Remembered by the history books as a great adventurer and the ultimate underdog, Houdini remains an inspiration to young entertainers throughout the world.

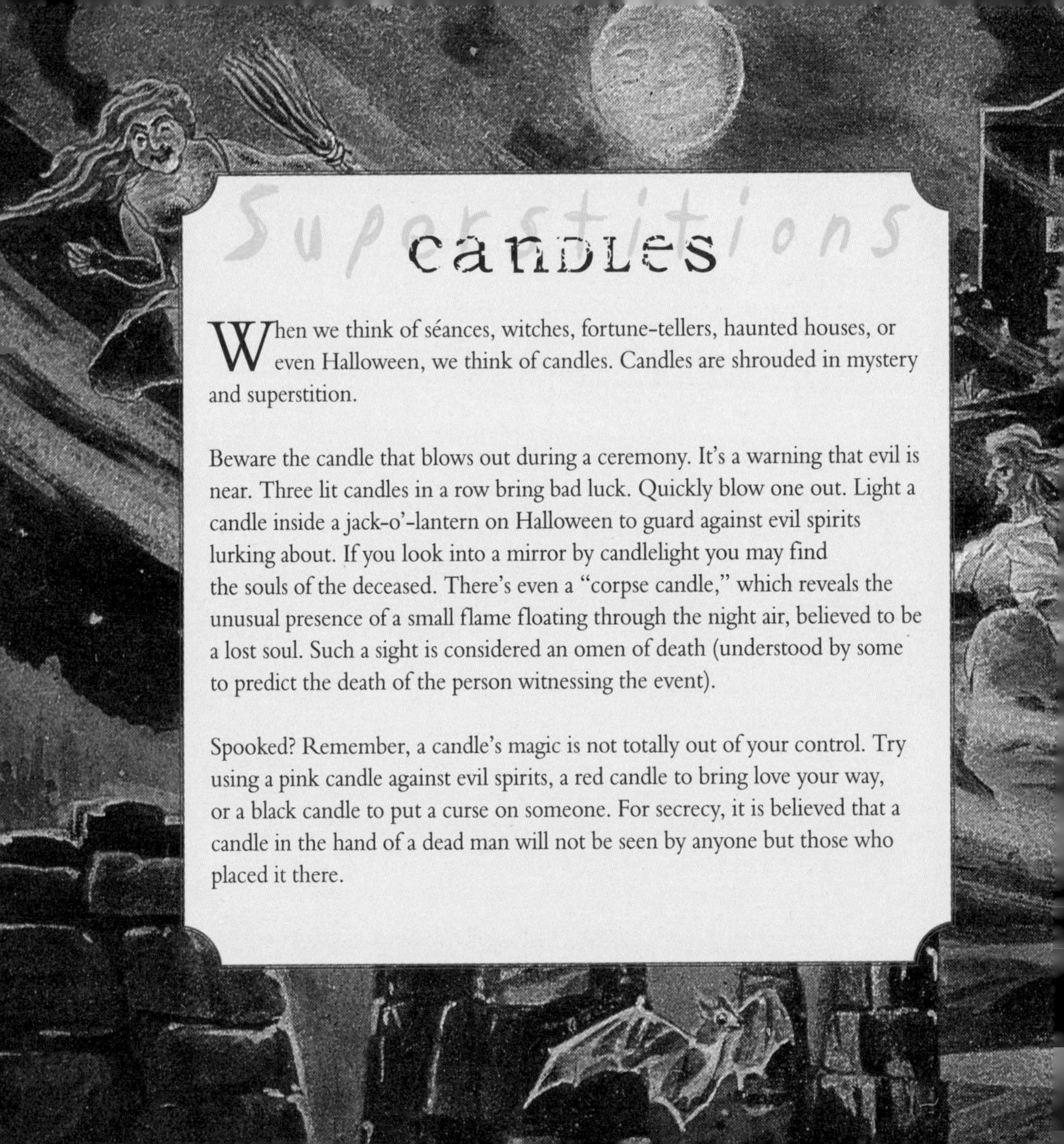

Candles

When we think of séances, witches, fortune-tellers, haunted houses, or even Halloween, we think of candles. Candles are shrouded in mystery and superstition.

Beware the candle that blows out during a ceremony. It's a warning that evil is near. Three lit candles in a row bring bad luck. Quickly blow one out. Light a candle inside a jack-o'-lantern on Halloween to guard against evil spirits lurking about. If you look into a mirror by candlelight you may find the souls of the deceased. There's even a "corpse candle," which reveals the unusual presence of a small flame floating through the night air, believed to be a lost soul. Such a sight is considered an omen of death (understood by some to predict the death of the person witnessing the event).

Spooked? Remember, a candle's magic is not totally out of your control. Try using a pink candle against evil spirits, a red candle to bring love your way, or a black candle to put a curse on someone. For secrecy, it is believed that a candle in the hand of a dead man will not be seen by anyone but those who placed it there.

THE CURSE OF KING TUT'S TOMB

For centuries, thieves broke into the tombs in Egypt's Valley of the Kings and ran off with gold and treasures. Modern-day archeologist Howard Carter was certain that one untouched tomb remained to be found—the final resting place of King Tutankhamon. The mysterious young Pharaoh, who reigned more than 3,300 years ago, died at the age of 18 and his tomb had never been found. For 30 years, Carter was obsessed in his search, but by 1922 his luck was running out. Lord Carnarvon, Carter's wealthy friend who funded his digs in the desert sands, had lost a fortune and didn't want to spend another dime. But Carter begged for one last chance, and he got it. He started digging in the last unexplored part of the Valley, and in November of 1922 uncovered a descending staircase. Frantic with excitement, Carter cabled Lord Carnarvon to fly down from England and join him in uncovering the tomb.

On November 26, 1922, Carter scraped a hole through the doorway to King Tutankhamon's tomb and lit a candle at the opening. Carnarvon stood beside him, restless for the news. "Can you see anything?" Carnarvon asked anxiously.

"Yes," said Carter, barely able to speak, "wonderful things. . . ." Over the next few days they broke through the sealed doors and found rooms filled with gold statues, furniture, jewelry, and other priceless objects. Carter and Carnarvon also found a frightening message on a clay tablet. They swiftly hid it away, fearing the Egyptian workers would flee if they learned of it. The inscription was a warning and a curse:

> DEATH WILL SLAY WITH HIS WINGS WHOEVER DISTURBS THE PEACE OF THE PHARAOH

King Tut's tomb soon proved to be the greatest archeological discovery of all time. The curse—which reached the newspapers after Carnarvon sold the story—became the most famous in history as headlines around the world announced "The Curse of the Pharaohs." The curse's first victim was Lord Carnarvon, who died of an unknown disease just five months after the discovery. An American journalist who helped unseal the tomb fell into a coma and died shortly after Carnarvon. A friend of Carnarvon came to visit the tomb and died the next day. A radiologist who took x-rays of King Tut's mummy died after returning to England. The death toll continued to climb, and by 1929 the curse had claimed 22 lives. Oddly, Howard Carter survived the curse and died of natural causes in 1939 at the age of 64.

EYEBALL COOKIES

1/2 cup shortening
1/4 cup brown sugar
1/2 teaspoon vanilla extract
1 cup flour
1/4 teaspoon salt
1 egg yolk
1/4 teaspoon full moon water
(see page 10)
Nutello, peanut butter, fruit jelly, and your choice of small round candies

1. Preheat oven to 375° & grease a cookie sheet.
2. In a cast iron cauldron or large bowl, mix shortening, brown sugar, vanilla extract, flour, and salt all together until it forms a dough.
3. In a separate bowl, beat egg white and moon water.
4. Roll dough into walnut sized balls and dip each one into egg white mixture. Place on a cookie sheet 2" apart.
5. Bake cookies for 5 minutes. Remove from oven and make thumbprint in each cookie. Bake for another 10 minutes.
6. Cool cookies on tray and fill each thumbprint with Nutello, peanut butter, or your favorite fruit jelly. Then place a chocolate chip or other candy of your choice in the center to complete the eyeball.

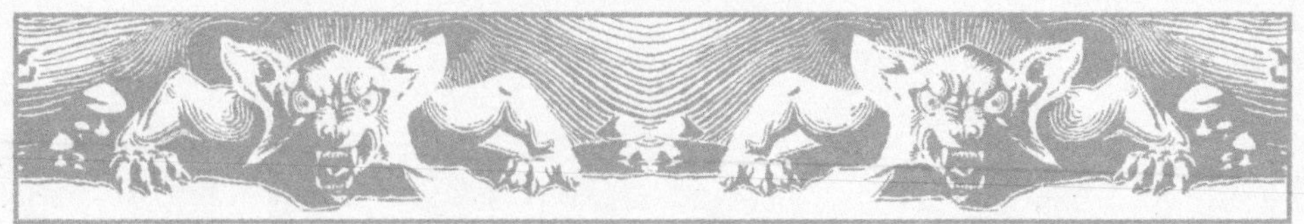

The Crystal Ball

adapted from the brothers Grimm

Once upon a time there was a nasty old witch who had three lovely sons. Though the boys were always kind, gentle, and honest, their evil mother suspected them of treachery and betrayal. Fearing they would steal her magical powers, the witch cast a spell on each of her children on their eighteenth birthdays, transforming them into wild animals. The eldest son became an eagle, doomed to spend his days soaring high above the rocky mountains. The middle son was turned into a whale and swam off to roam the ocean blue. But, the youngest son was determined to avoid his brothers' fate. So on the eve of his eighteenth birthday, he waited until he heard his wretched mother snoring in her bedroom and then sneaked away with just a few saved coins and a belted dagger.

The young man wandered from town to town, performing odd jobs in exchange for a meal or a barn floor to sleep on. One evening, as he treated himself to a cool summer brew in a local pub, he overheard two farmers speak of a beautiful young princess in a distant land whose father had hidden her away in a remote castle. The king, they said, had ordered the royal magician to cast a spell on the princess, altering her appearance to that of a hag. His Royal Highness then challenged the

twenty-four strongest bachelors of the land to try and break the curse. The first to succeed would win his daughter's hand and the key to the kingdom. But failure promised certain death, and already twenty-three potential suitors had fallen. Only one more would have the chance to save the young princess from a life of misery and loneliness.

Fearless and with a great love of adventure, the young witch's son vowed to find the princess and break the terrible curse. But there was one great obstacle in his way—he had no idea where she was hidden. So he began wandering the land, searching for the young lady who had already captured his heart, even though they had never met. After weeks of travel, the young man was beginning to lose hope when he came upon two giants fighting in a forest. As he approached the giants, they stopped wrestling and stood up.

"Kind sir," said one of the giants," would you help us resolve an argument? You see, we are fighting over this cap I'm holding. But we are equally strong and after three days, neither of us has won. Will you choose which one of us is the stronger?"

"Why should you fight so hard over a dirty old hat?" asked the young man.

"Oh, no," said the other giant shaking his head. "This is a very special cap. The one who wears it will be granted any wish he makes."

"Ah, that is special," replied the man. "Alright then. I'll put the cap on and stand by that old oak over there. Whoever reaches me first and grabs the hat will win it."

The giants agreed to the race and the young man set off toward the tree. But with each step he began to forget all about the quarreling giants and his mind wandered again to the cursed princess. For the hundredth time he wished he could find the castle that imprisoned his true love. Then before he knew it, there was a loud BANG! and he found himself standing at the foot of a mountain staring up at a beautiful castle glistening in the summer sun.

Dazed for a moment the young man realized what had just happened. "I've found my princess!" he cried, and began scrambling up the hill. It took all afternoon, but the young man finally reached the Princess' room at the top of the castle's highest tower. As he pushed open the door he flinched at the sight of the woman he had dreamed of all these months. She was the ugliest person he had ever seen! Her face was covered with warts and her skin hung from her bones like an old woman. Tufts of hair clung to her head and her teeth were the color of mildew. But before he could speak, the princess said quickly, "I am not the woman you see before you. Come look at my reflection in this mirror and you will see my true form."

The witch's son gazed into the mirror. There he saw a beautiful maiden with long auburn hair, creamy white skin and eyes the color of the sea.

"You see," she said, "this is the girl I was before my father had this terrible curse put on me."

"Madam," said the young man," I have come to free you."

"Kind sir, it is too dangerous. You seem to be a gentle and sweet man. I cannot allow you to risk your life for me. Twenty-three lives have already been lost."

"I am not afraid. Tell me simply what I must to do and I will succeed."

"At the bottom of this mountain you will find an angry bull. Kill the bull and a beautiful red raven will fly from its stomach. The raven holds in its claws a magical crystal ball. You must capture that ball and hold it up before the Royal Magician in order to break my curse. But beware, the raven won't give up the crystal willingly. And if the ball hits the ground, it will burst into flames and devour everything for a mile around."

"Fair maiden," said the young man bowing, "I will return for you before the moon shows its face." He kissed the princess' haggard hand and left to face his challenge.

As the young man reached the bottom of the mountain, he came face to face with the angry bull. The bull put up a bitter fight, but the young man finally triumphed as he plunged his dagger deep into the animal's heart. Sure enough, a raven holding the crystal ball in its claws sprung forth from the gut of the bull and soared high into the clouds above. But the young man's eldest brother, now a full-grown eagle, had been flying by overhead. The magnificent bird swooped down, ferociously attacking the raven with his massive beak. The raven dropped the crystal ball as it tried to escape and the ball landed on the roof a

fisherman's hut by the shore. It began to smoke and was about to explode, when a huge wave rose up and washed over the hut, extinguishing the burning crystal. This was the handiwork of the young man's other brother, the mighty whale! As he swam nearby, the whale had thrashed his massive body around in the surf in order to create a wall of water that rose and crashed into the shore.

The young man cried out," Thank you brothers!" and raced to pick up the crystal ball. Hours later he held up the magic crystal before the Royal Magician, and broke the princess' curse forever. When he returned to the castle he found his true love weeping in her room.

"My dear princess," the young man said soothingly, "what is the reason for your tears. The curse has been broken. I thought you would be bursting with joy."

"My lord, these are tears of pure happiness. I never allowed myself to believe I would be freed. You are truly my hero and I will love you until the end of time."

The young man lifted up his princess and kissed her passionately on the lips. Later that evening they exchanged their marriage vows beneath a full moon on the ocean's shore. And as the royal priest pronounced them husband and wife, an eagle cooed from high above and the sound of whale song filled the air. ☾

If You See a Fairy Ring

by Anonymous

If you see a fairy ring
In a field of grass,
Very lightly step around,
Tiptoe as you pass;
Last night fairies frolicked there,
And they're sleeping somewhere near.

If you see a tiny fairy
Lying fast asleep,
Shut your eyes and run away,
Do not stay to peep;
And be sure you never tell,
Or you'll break a fairy spell.

A Spell to Dream True

It is well known among modern witches and sorcerers that dreams are useful tools for foretelling the future. To inspire psychic dreams, stuff your pillow with the leaves of the weed-like mugwort plant. Using this dream pillow to inspire prophecy dates back to ancient magical times. Always sleep alone when using a Mugwort pillow and keep a pad and pencil handy to jot down your visions as soon as you wake. If you cannot gather enough of the herb to fill your pillow, just a few dried leaves burned as incense should do the trick quite nicely.

ARE YOU DEAD OR ALIVE?

Command your heartbeat to stop and start again with this easy yet amazing trick.

Bunch up a hand towel into a hard ball and secretly place it under your arm.

Insert a thumbtack into the end of a wooden match stick. Place this on your wrist over your pulse.

Ask your audience to step up and take a close look at the moving match stick. With each heartbeat, the match shakes.

Point at the match and say, "Abracadabra—STOP!" At the same time, tightly squeeze the towel under your arm.

The pressure has slowed down the blood flow to your wrist, and the match no longer moves. Invite your audience to look closely, saying, "My heart has stopped at my command."

Then say, "I command you to COME TO LIFE!" Relax your arm and let the blood flow strongly again. The match will immediately start to move with your pulse.

HARRY

BY ROSEMARY TIMPERLEY

uch ordinary things make me afraid. Sunshine. Sharp shadows on grass. White roses. Children with red hair. And the name—Harry. Such an ordinary name.

Yet the first time Christine mentioned the name, I felt a premonition of fear.

She was five years old, due to start school in three months' time. It was a hot, beautiful day and she was playing alone in the garden, as she often did. I saw her lying on her stomach in the grass, picking daisies and making daisy-chains with laborious pleasure. The sun burned on her pale red hair and made her skin look very white. Her big blue eyes were wide with concentration.

Suddenly she looked towards the bush of white roses, which cast its shadow over the grass, and smiled.

"Yes, I'm Christine," she said. She rose and walked slowly towards the bush, her little plump legs defenseless and endearing beneath the too short blue cotton skirt. She was growing fast.

"With my mummy and daddy," she said clearly. Then, after a pause, "Oh, but they *are* my mummy and daddy."

She was in the shadow of the bush now. It was as if she'd walked

out of the world of light into darkness. Uneasy, without quite knowing why, I called her:

"Chris, what are you doing?"

"Nothing." The voice sounded too far away.

"Come indoors now. It's too hot for you out there."

"Not too hot."

"Come indoors, Chris."

She said: "I must go in now. Goodbye," then walked slowly towards the house.

"Chris, who were you talking to?"

"Harry," she said.

"Who's Harry?"

"Harry."

I couldn't get anything else out of her, so I just gave her some cake and milk and read to her until bedtime. As she listened, she stared out at the garden. Once she smiled and waved. It was a relief finally to tuck her up in bed and feel she was safe.

When Jim, my husband, came home I told him about the mysterious "Harry." He laughed.

"Oh, she's started that lark, has she?"

"What do you mean, Jim?"

"It's not so very rare for only children to have an imaginary companion. Some kids talk to their dolls. Chris has never been keen on her dolls. She hasn't any brothers or sisters. She hasn't any friends

her own age. So she imagines someone."

"But why has she picked that particular name?"

He shrugged. "You know how kids pick things up. I don't know what you're worrying about, honestly I don't."

"Nor do I really. It's just that I feel extra responsible for her. More so than if I were her real mother."

"I know, but she's all right. Chris is fine. She's a pretty, healthy, intelligent little girl. A credit to you."

"And to you."

"In fact, we're thoroughly nice parents!"

"And so modest!"

We laughed together and he kissed me. I felt consoled.

Until next morning.

Again the sun shone brilliantly on the small, bright lawn and white roses. Christine was sitting on the grass, cross-legged, staring towards the rose bush, smiling.

"Hello," she said. "I hoped you'd come . . . Because I like you. How old are you? . . . I'm only five and a piece . . . I'm *not* a baby! I'm going to school soon and I shall have a new dress. A green one. Do you go to school? . . . What do you do then?" She was silent for a while, nodding, listening, absorbed.

I felt myself going cold as I stood there in the kitchen. "Don't be silly. Lots of children have an imaginary companion," I told myself desperately. "Just carry on as if nothing were happening. Don't listen.

Don't be a fool."

But I called Chris in earlier than usual for her mid-morning milk.

"Your milk's ready, Chris. Come along."

"In a minute." This was a strange reply. Usually she rushed in eagerly for her milk and the special sandwich cream biscuits, over which she was a little gourmande.

"Come now, darling," I said.

"Can Harry come too?"

"No!" The cry burst from me harshly, surprising me.

"Goodbye, Harry. I'm sorry you can't come in but I've got to have my milk," Chris said, then ran towards the house.

"Why can't Harry have some milk too?" she challenged me.

"Who *is* Harry, darling?"

"Harry's my brother."

"But Chris, you haven't got a brother. Daddy and mummy have only got one child, one little girl, that's you. Harry can't be your brother."

"Harry's my brother. He says so." She bent over the glass of milk and emerged with a smeary top lip. Then she grabbed at the biscuits. At least "Harry" hadn't spoilt her appetite!

After she'd had her milk, I said, "We'll go shopping now, Chris. You'd like to come to the shops with me, wouldn't you?"

"I want to stay with Harry."

"Well you can't. You're coming with me."

"Can Harry come too?"

"No."

My hands were trembling as I put on my hat and gloves. It was chilly in the house nowadays, as if there were a cold shadow over it in spite of the sun outside. Chris came with me meekly enough, but as we walked down the street, she turned and waved.

I didn't mention any of this to Jim that night. I knew he'd only scoff as he'd done before. But when Christine's "Harry" fantasy went on day after day, it got more and more on my nerves. I came to hate and dread those long summer days. I longed for grey skies and rain. I longed for the white roses to wither and die. I trembled when I heard Christine's voice prattling away in the garden. She talked quite unrestrainedly to "Harry" now.

One Sunday, when Jim heard her at it, he said:

"I'll say one thing for imaginary companions, they help a child on with her talking. Chris is talking much more freely than she used to."

"With an accent," I blurted out.

"An accent?"

"A slight cockney accent."

"My dearest, every London child gets a slight cockney accent. It'll be much worse when she goes to school and meets lots of other kids."

"We don't talk cockney. Where does she get if from? Who can she be getting it from except Ha . . ." I couldn't say the name.

"The baker, the milkman, the dustman, the coalman, the window cleaner—want any more?"

"I suppose not." I laughed ruefully. Jim made me feel foolish.

"Anyway," said Jim, "*I* haven't noticed any cockney in her voice."

"There isn't when she talks to us. It's only when she's talking to—to him."

"To Harry. You know, I'm getting quite attached to young Harry. Wouldn't it be fun if one day we looked out and saw him?"

"Don't!" I cried. "Don't say that! It's my nightmare. My waking nightmare. Oh, Jim, I can't bear it much longer."

He looked astonished. "This Harry business is really getting you down, isn't it?"

"Of course it is! Day in, day out, I hear nothing but 'Harry this,' 'Harry that,' 'Harry says,' 'Harry thinks,' 'Can Harry have some?,' 'Can Harry come too?'—it's all right for you out at the office all day, but I have to live with it: I'm—I'm afraid of it, Jim. It's so queer."

"Do you know what I think you should do to put your mind at rest?"

"What?"

"Take Chris along to see old Dr. Webster tomorrow. Let him have a little talk with her."

"Do you think she's ill—in her mind?"

"Good heavens, no! But when we come across something that's a bit beyond us, it's as well to take professional advice."

Next day I took Chris to see Dr. Webster. I left her in the waiting-room while I told him briefly about Harry. He nodded sympa-

thetically, then said:

"It's a fairly unusual case, Mrs. James, but by no means unique. I've had several cases of children's imaginary companions becoming so real to them that the parents got the jitters. I expect she's rather a lonely little girl, isn't she?"

"She doesn't know any other children. We're new to the neighbourhood, you see. But that will be put right when she starts school."

"And I think you'll find that when she goes to school and meets other children, these fantasies will disappear. You see, every child needs company of her own age, and if she doesn't get it, she invents it. Older people who are lonely talk to themselves. That doesn't mean that they're crazy, just that they need to talk to someone. A child is more practical. Seems silly to talk to oneself, she thinks, so she invents someone to talk to. I honestly don't think you've anything to worry about."

"That's what my husband says."

"I'm sure he does. Still, I'll have a chat with Christine as you've brought her. Leave us alone together."

I went to the waiting-room to fetch Chris. She was at the window. She said: "Harry's waiting."

"Where, Chris?" I said quietly, wanting suddenly to see with her eyes.

"There. By the rose bush."

The doctor had a bush of white roses in his garden.

"There's no one there," I said. Chris gave me a glance of unchild-like scorn. "Dr. Webster wants to see you now, darling," I said shakily. "You remember him, don't you? He gave you sweets when you were getting better from chicken pox."

"Yes," she said and went willingly enough to the doctor's surgery. I waited restlessly. Faintly I heard their voices through the wall, heard the doctor's chuckle, Christine's high peal of laughter. She was talking away to the doctor in a way she didn't talk to me.

When they came out, he said: "Nothing wrong with her whatever. She's just an imaginative little monkey. A word of advice, Mrs. James. Let her talk about Harry. Let her become accustomed to confiding in you. I gather you've shown some disapproval of this "brother" of hers so she doesn't talk much to you about him. He makes wooden toys, doesn't he, Chris?"

"Yes, Harry makes wooden toys."

"And he can read and write, can't he?"

"And swim and climb trees and paint pictures. Harry can do everything. He's a wonderful brother." Her little face flushed with adoration.

The doctor patted me on the shoulder and said: "Harry sounds a very nice brother for her. He's even got red hair like you, Chris, hasn't he?"

"Harry's got red hair," said Chris proudly, "Redder than my hair. And he's nearly as tall as daddy only thinner. He's as tall as you, mummy. He's fourteen. He says he's tall for his age. What *is* tall for his age?"

"Mummy will tell you about that as you walk home," said Dr. Webster. "Now, goodbye, Mrs. James. Don't worry. Just let her prattle. Goodbye, Chris. Give my love to Harry."

"He's there," said Chris, pointing to the doctor's garden. "He's been waiting for me."

Dr. Webster laughed. "They're incorrigible, aren't they?" he said. "I knew one poor mother whose children invented a whole tribe of imaginary natives whose rituals and taboos ruled the household. Perhaps you're lucky, Mrs. James!"

I tried to feel comforted by all this, but I wasn't. I hoped sincerely that when Chris started school this wretched Harry business would finish.

Chris ran ahead of me. She looked up as if at someone beside her. For a brief, dreadful second, I saw a shadow on the pavement alongside her own—a long, thin shadow—like a boy's shadow. Then it was gone. I ran to catch her up and held her hand tightly all the way home. Even in the comparative security of the house—the house so strangely cold in this hot weather—I never let her out of my sight. On the face of it she behaved no differently towards me, but in reality she was drifting away. The child in my house was becoming a stranger.

For the first time since Jim and I had adopted Chris, I wondered seriously: Who is she? Where does she come from? Who were her real

parents? Who is this little loved stranger I've taken as a daughter? Who *is* Christine?

Another week passed. It was Harry, Harry all the time. The day before she was to start school, Chris said:

"Not going to school."

"You're going to school tomorrow, Chris. You're looking forward to it. You know you are. There'll be lots of other little girls and boys."

"Harry says he can't come too."

"You won't want Harry at school. He'll—" I tried hard to follow the doctor's advice and appear to believe in Harry—"He'll be too old. He'd feel silly among little boys and girls, and great lad of fourteen."

"I won't go to school without Harry. I want to be with Harry." She began to weep, loudly, painfully.

"Chris, stop this nonsense! Stop it!" I struck her sharply on the arm. Her crying ceased immediately. She stared at me, her blue eyes wide open and frighteningly cold. She gave me an adult stare that made me tremble. Then she said:

"You don't love me. Harry loves me. Harry wants me. He says I can go with him."

"I will not hear any more of this!" I shouted, hating the anger in my voice, hating myself for being angry at all with a little girl—*my* little girl—mine—

I went down on one knee and held out my arms.

"Chris, darling, come here."

She came, slowly. "I love you," I said. "I love you, Chris, and I'm real. School is real. Go to school to please me."

"Harry will go away if I do."

"You'll have other friends."

"I want Harry." Again the tears, wet against my shoulder now. I held her closely.

"You're tired, baby. Come to bed."

She slept with the tear stains still on her face.

It was still daylight. I went to the window to draw her curtains. Golden shadows and long strips of sunshine in the garden. Then, again like a dream, the long thin clear-cut shadow of a boy near the white roses. Like a mad woman I opened the window and shouted:

"Harry! Harry!"

I thought I saw a glimmer of red among the roses, like close red curls on a boy's head. Then there was nothing.

When I told Jim about Christine's emotional outburst he said: "Poor little kid. It's always a nervy business, starting school. She'll be all right once she gets there. You'll be hearing less about Harry too, as time goes on."

"Harry doesn't want her to go to school."

"Hey! You sound as if you believe in Harry yourself!"

"Sometimes I do."

"Believing in evil spirits in your old age?" he teased me. But his eyes were concerned. He thought I was going 'round the bend" and

small blame to him!

"I don't think Harry's evil," I said. "He's just a boy. A boy who doesn't exist, except for Christine. And who *is* Christine?"

"None of that!" said Jim sharply. "When we adopted Chris we decided she was to be our own child. No probing into the past. No wondering and worrying. No mysteries. Chris is as much ours as if she'd been born of our flesh. Who is Christine indeed! She's our daughter—and just you remember that!"

"Yes, Jim, you're right. Of course you're right."

He'd been so fierce about it that I didn't tell him what I planned to do the next day while Chris was at school.

Next morning Chris was silent and sulky. Jim joked with her and tried to cheer her, but all she would do was look out of the window and say: "Harry's gone."

"You won't need Harry now. You're going to school," said Jim.

Chris gave him that look of grown-up contempt she'd given me sometimes.

She and I didn't speak as I took her to school. I was almost in tears. Although I was glad for her to start school, I felt a sense of loss at parting with her. I suppose every mother feels that when she takes her ewe-lamb to school for the first time. It's the end of babyhood for the child, the beginning of life in reality, life with its cruelty, its strangeness, its barbarity. I kissed her goodbye at the gate and said:

"You'll be having dinner at school with the other children,

Chris, and I'll call for you when school is over, at three o'clock."

"Yes, mummy." She held my hand tightly. Other nervous little children were arriving with equally nervous parents. A pleasant young teacher with fair hair and a white linen dress appeared at the gate. She gathered the new children towards her and led them away. She gave me a sympathetic smile as she passed and said: "We'll take good care of her."

I felt quite light-hearted as I walked away, knowing that Chris was safe and I didn't have to worry.

Now I started on my secret mission. I took a bus to town and went to the big, gaunt building I hadn't visited for over five years. Then, Jim and I had gone together. The top floor of the building belonged to the Greythorne Adoption Society. I climbed the four flights and knocked on the familiar door with its scratched paint. A secretary whose face I didn't know let me in.

"May I see Miss Cleaver? My name is Mrs. James."

"Have you an appointment?"

"No, but it's very important."

"I'll see," The girl went out and returned a second later. "Miss Cleaver will see you, Mrs. James."

Miss Cleaver, a tall, thin, grey haired woman with a charming smile, a plain, kindly face and a very wrinkled brow, rose to meet me. "Mrs. James. How nice to see you again. How's Christine?"

"She's very well. Miss Cleaver, I'd better get straight to the point. I know you don't normally divulge the origin of a child to its adopters and vice versa, but I must know who Christine is."

"Sorry, Mrs. James," she began, "our rules . . ."

"Please let me tell you the whole story, then you'll see I'm not just suffering from vulgar curiosity."

I told her about Harry.

When I'd finished, she said: "It's very queer. Very queer indeed. Mrs. James, I'm going to break my rule for once. I'm going to tell you in strict confidence where Christine came from.

"She was born in a very poor part of London. There were four in the family, father, mother, son and Christine herself."

"Son?"

"Yes. He was fourteen when—when it happened."

"When what happened?"

"Let me start at the beginning. The parents hadn't really wanted Christine. The family lived in one room at the top of an old house which should have been condemned by the Sanitary Inspector in my opinion. It was difficult enough when there were only three of them, but with a baby as well life became a nightmare. The mother was a neurotic creature, slatternly, unhappy, too fat. After she'd had the baby she took no interest in it. The brother, however, adored the little girl from the start. He got into trouble for cutting school so he could look after her.

"The father had a steady job in a warehouse, not much money,

but enough to keep them alive. Then he was sick for several weeks and lost his job. He was laid up in that messy room, ill, worrying, nagged by his wife, irked by the baby's crying and his son's eternal fussing over the child—I got all these details from neighbours afterwards, by the way. I was also told that he'd had a particularly bad time in the war and had been in a nerve hospital for several months before he was fit to come home at all after his demob. Suddenly it all proved too much for him.

"One morning, in the small hours, a woman in the ground floor room saw something fall past her window and heard a thud on the ground. She went out to look. The son of the family was there on the ground. Christine was in his arms. The boy's neck was broken. He was dead. Christine was blue in the face but still breathing faintly.

"The woman woke the household, sent for the police and the doctor, then they went to the top room. They had to break down the door, which was locked and sealed inside. An overpowering smell of gas greeted them, in spite of the open window.

"They found husband and wife dead in bed and a note from the husband saying:

'I can't go on. I am going to kill them all. It's the only way.'

"The police concluded that he'd sealed up door and windows and turned on the gas when his family were asleep, then lain beside his wife until he drifted into unconsciousness, and death. But the son must have

wakened. Perhaps he struggled with the door but couldn't open it. He'd be too weak to shout. All he could do was pluck away the seals from the window, open it, and fling himself out, holding his adored little sister tightly in his arms.

"Why Christine herself wasn't gassed is rather a mystery. Perhaps her head was right under the bedclothes, pressed against her brother's chest—they always slept together. Anyway, the child was taken to hospital, then to the home where you and Mr. James first saw her . . . and a lucky day that was for little Christine!"

"So her brother saved her life and died himself?" I said.

"Yes. He was a very brave young man."

"Perhaps he thought not so much of saving her as of keeping her with him. Oh dear! That sounds ungenerous. I didn't mean to be. Miss Cleaver, what was his name?"

"I'll have to look that up for you." She referred to one of her many files and said at last: "The family's name was Jones and the fourteen-year-old brother was called 'Harold.'"

"And did he have red hair?" I murmured.

"That I don't know, Mrs. James."

"But it's Harry. The boy was Harry. What does it mean? I can't understand it."

"It's not easy, but I think perhaps deep in her unconscious mind Christine has always remembered Harry, the companion of her babyhood. We don't think of children as having much memory, but there must be images of the past tucked away somewhere in their little heads. Christine doesn't *invent* this Harry. She *remembers* him. So clearly that she's almost brought him to life again. I know it sounds farfetched, but the whole story is so odd that I can't think of any other explanation."

"May I have the address of the house where they lived?"

She was reluctant to give me this information, but I persuaded her and set out at last to find No. 13 Canver Row, where the man Jones had tried to kill himself and his whole family and almost succeeded.

The house seemed deserted. It was filthy and derelict. But one thing made me stare and stare. There was a tiny garden. A scatter of bright uneven grass splashed the bald brown patches of earth. But the little garden had one strange glory that none of the other houses in the poor sad street possessed—a bush of white roses. They bloomed gloriously. Their scent was overpowering.

I stood by the bush and stared up at the top window.

A voice startled me: "What are you doing here?"

It was an old woman, peering from the ground floor window.

"I thought the house was empty," I said.

"Should be. Been condemned. But they can't get me out. Nowhere else to go. Won't go. The others went quickly enough after it hap-

pened. No one else wants to come. They say the place is haunted. So it is. But what's the fuss about? Life and death. They're very close. You get to know that when you're old. Alive or dead. What's the difference?"

She looked at me with yellowish, bloodshot eyes and said: "I saw him fall past my window. That's where he fell. Among the roses. He still comes back. I see him. He won't go away until he gets her."

"Who—who are you talking about?"

"Harry Jones. Nice boy he was. Red hair. Very thin. Too determined though. Always got his own way. Loved Christine too much I thought. Died among the roses. Used to sit down here with her for hours, by the roses. Then died there. Or do people die? The church ought to give us an answer, but it doesn't. Not one you can believe. Go away, will you? This place isn't for you. It's for the dead who aren't dead, and the living who aren't alive. Am I alive or dead? You tell me. I don't know."

The crazy eyes staring at me beneath the matted white fringe of hair frightened me. Mad people are terrifying. One can pity them, but one is still afraid. I murmured:

"I'll go now. Goodbye," and tried to hurry across the hard hot pavements although my legs felt heavy and half-paralyzed, as in a nightmare.

The sun blazed down on my head, but I was hardly aware of it. I lost all sense of time or place as I stumbled on.

Then I heard something that chilled my blood.

A clock struck three.

At three o'clock I was supposed to be at the school gates, waiting for Christine.

Where was I now? How near the school? What bus should I take?

I made frantic inquiries of passers-by, who looked at me fearfully, as I had looked at the old woman. They must have thought I was crazy.

At last I caught the right bus and, sick with dust, petrol fumes and fear, reached the school. I ran across the hot, empty playground. In a classroom, the young teacher in white was gathering her books together.

"I've come for Christine James. I'm her mother. I'm so sorry I'm late. Where is she?" I gasped.

"Christine James?" The girl frowned, then said brightly: "Oh, yes, I remember, the pretty little red-haired girl. That's all right, Mrs. James. Her brother called for her. How alike they are, aren't they? And so devoted. It's rather sweet to see a boy of that age so fond of his baby sister. Has your husband got red hair, like the two children?"

"What did—her brother—say?" I asked faintly.

"He didn't say anything. When I spoke to him, he just smiled. They'll be home by now, I should think. I say, do you feel all right?"

"Yes, thank you. I must go home."

I ran all the way home through the burning streets.

"Chris! Christine, where are you? Chris! Chris!" Sometimes even now I hear my own voice of the past screaming through the cold

house. "Christine! Chris! Where are you? Answer me! Chrrriiiiiss!" Then: "Harry! Don't take her away! Come back! Harry! Harry!"

Demented, I rushed out into the garden. The sun struck me like a hot blade. The roses glared whitely. The air was so still I seemed to stand in timelessness, placelessness. For a moment, I seemed very near to Christine, although I couldn't see her. Then the roses danced before my eyes and turned red. The world turned red. Blood red. Wet red. I fell through redness to blackness to nothingness—to almost death.

For weeks I was in bed with sunstroke which turned to brain fever. During that time Jim and the police searched for Christine in vain. The futile search continued for months. The papers were full of the strange disappearance of the red-haired child. The teacher described the "brother" who had called for her. There were newspaper stories of kidnapping, baby-snatching, child-murders.

Then the sensation died down. Just another unsolved mystery in police files.

And only two people knew what had happened. An old crazed woman living in a derelict house, and myself.

Years have passed. But I walk in fear.

Such ordinary things make me afraid. Sunshine. Sharp shadows on grass. White roses. Children with red hair. And the name—Harry. Such an ordinary name!

The Vampire

by Rudyard Kipling

A fool there was and he made his prayer
(Even as you and I!)
To a rag and a bone and a hank of hair
(We called her the woman who
did not care)
But the fool he called her his lady fair—
(Even as you and I!)

Oh, the years we waste and the tears
we waste
And the work of our head and hand
Belong to the woman who did not know
(And now we know that she
never could know)
And did not understand!

A fool there was and his goods he spent
(Even as you and I!)
Honour and faith and a sure intent
(And it wasn't the least what the lady meant)

But a fool must follow his natural bent
(Even as you and I!)

Oh, the toil we lost and the spoil we lost
And the excellent things we planned
Belong to the woman who didn't know why
(And now we know that she never knew why)
And did not understand!

The fool was stripped to his foolish hide
(Even as you and I!)
Which she might have seen when she threw him aside—
(But it isn't on record the lady tried)
So some of him lived but the most of him died—
(Even as you and I!)

And it isn't the shame and it isn't the blame
That stings like a white-hot brand—
It's coming to know that she never knew why
(Seeing, at last, she could never know why)
And never could understand!

THE CURSE OF THE BURTON AGNES SKULL

When the Griffin family decided to build a new home on their Yorkshire lands in 1598, their three daughters took great interest in the project. Anne, in particular, followed every detail of constructing Burton Agnes Hall from start to finish, and grew very attached to the grand house after moving in.

One night, while returning from a visit to a neighbor, Anne was attacked on the road by a gang of thieves. She was struck in the head and, if not for her rescue by villagers who heard her screams, she would have died on the spot. She was brought home to the loving arms of her family, but the outlook was grim. Before dying, Anne begged her sisters to keep part of her in Burton Agnes Hall forever. In her final farewell, she asked them to have her skull buried within the walls of the house she had helped to build.

Anne died five days after the attack, and her family ignored her request by burying her—head and all—in the church

graveyard. Soon, blood-curdling screams began to ring out in Burton Agnes Hall. No one could discover their source. Alarmed and chilled to the bone in fear, the sisters feared that the screams were a ghostly call from Anne to fulfill her dying wish. The family, with no other solution in sight, decided to dig up Anne's grave and obey her wishes. When the coffin was opened, the small group received another grisly shock: the body had not decayed, but the head had fallen off and lost every bit of hair and tissue, leaving only a bare skull. The Griffins took the skull home and the screams stopped.

All was well for many years, until the house was sold to another family who banished the skull from the hall. The screams returned, much to the horror of the new inhabitants. Again the skull was returned, and all was quiet once more. Later, a new owner hid the skull away within a wall and never told anyone where it was hidden. No one has found the skull's hiding place to this day, and the screams have not returned. Some people have seen Anne floating through the house in October, the month in which she was killed. They recognize the ghost as Anne, as it matches her portrait, which hangs in the home to this day.

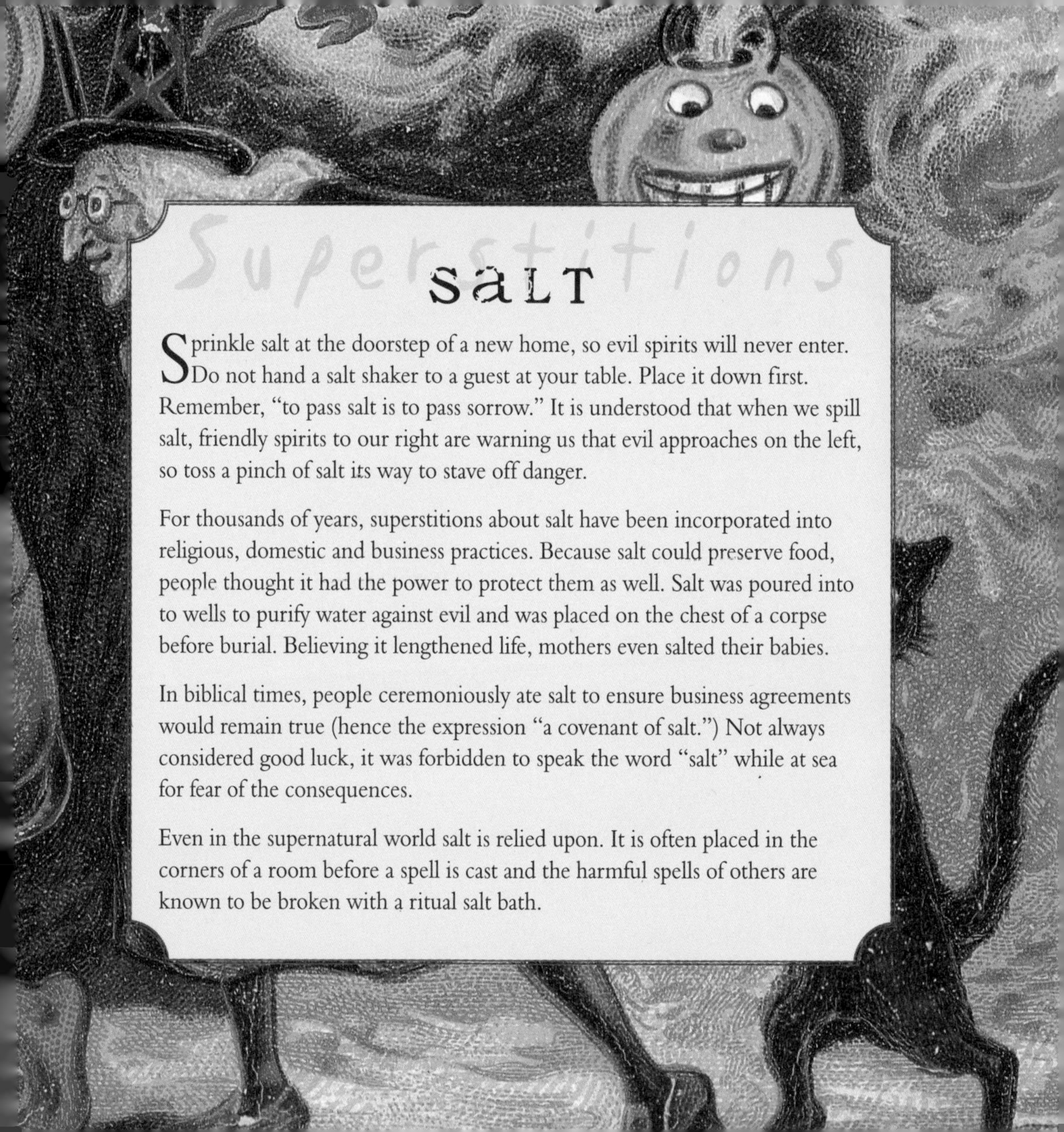

SALT

Sprinkle salt at the doorstep of a new home, so evil spirits will never enter. Do not hand a salt shaker to a guest at your table. Place it down first. Remember, "to pass salt is to pass sorrow." It is understood that when we spill salt, friendly spirits to our right are warning us that evil approaches on the left, so toss a pinch of salt its way to stave off danger.

For thousands of years, superstitions about salt have been incorporated into religious, domestic and business practices. Because salt could preserve food, people thought it had the power to protect them as well. Salt was poured into to wells to purify water against evil and was placed on the chest of a corpse before burial. Believing it lengthened life, mothers even salted their babies.

In biblical times, people ceremoniously ate salt to ensure business agreements would remain true (hence the expression "a covenant of salt.") Not always considered good luck, it was forbidden to speak the word "salt" while at sea for fear of the consequences.

Even in the supernatural world salt is relied upon. It is often placed in the corners of a room before a spell is cast and the harmful spells of others are known to be broken with a ritual salt bath.

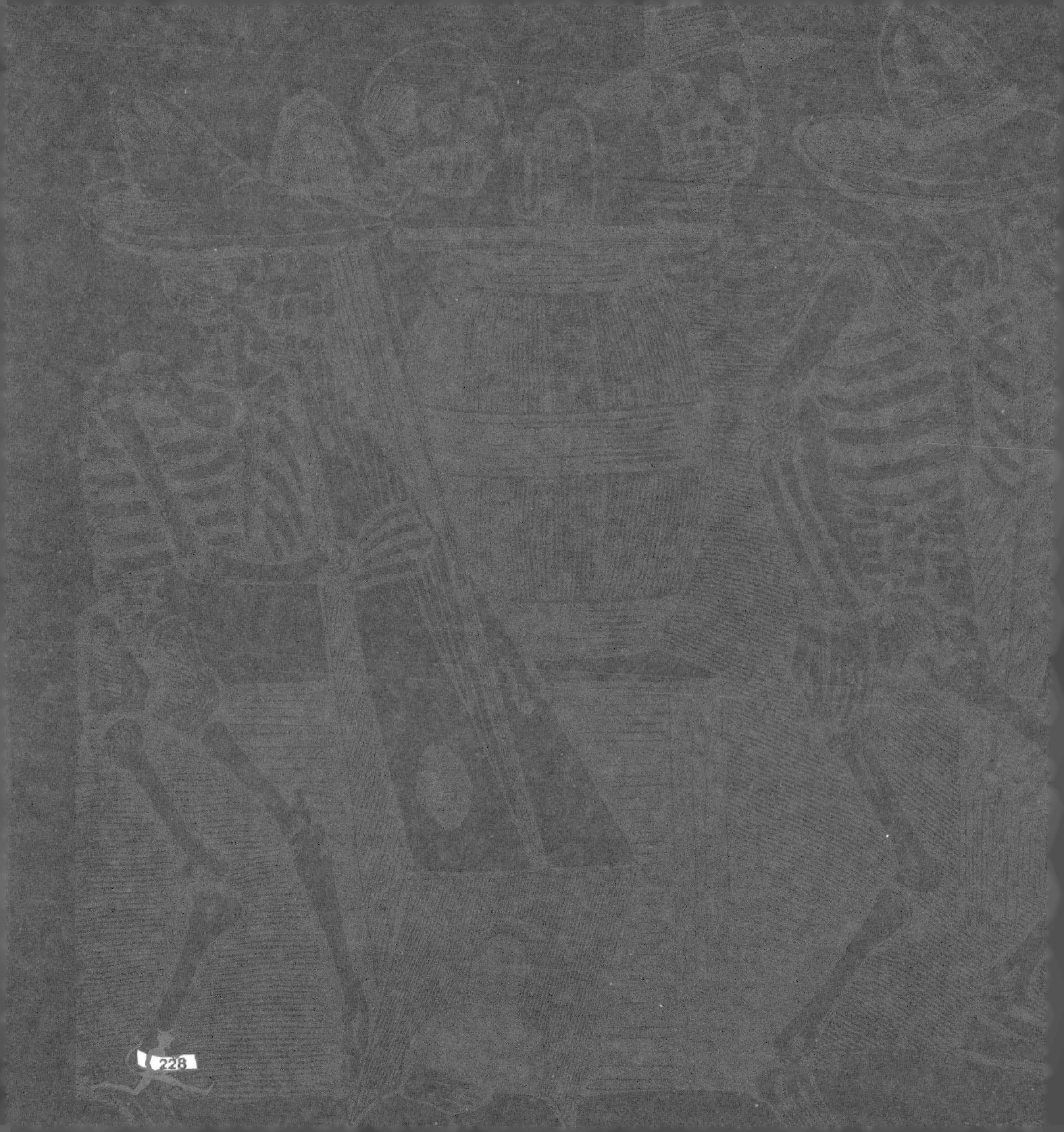

The Day of the Dead

The Day of the Dead is a traditional Mexican holiday that commemorates and honors the death of loved family members and friends. Despite its spooky name, the Day of the Dead is a festive celebration of devotion and remembrance, that lasts for two days in early November every year.

As the holiday approaches, families prepare altars in their homes by filling them with flowers, candles, and photos of lost loved ones. Symbolic gifts, such as breads or sugar skeletons are presented by friends and neighbors and added to the shrines. On November 1st, households throughout Mexico carry the contents of their altars to their local cemeteries where they spend the night at the gravesites of their lost relatives, telling stories and talking to the spirits of the dead. In the morning, the mourners return home in high spirits to celebrate with music and lavish feasts. As dusk sets in, doors and windows are pushed open so that any remaining spirits may wander in and join the revelry.

A GHOST STORY

BY MARK TWAIN

I took a large room, far up Broadway, in a huge old building whose upper stories had been wholly unoccupied for years, until I came. The place had long been given up to dust and cobwebs, to solitude and silence. I seemed groping among the tombs and invading the privacy of the dead, that first night I climbed up to my quarters. For the first time in my life a superstitious dread came over me; and as I turned a dark angle of the stairway and an invisible cobweb swung its slazy woof in my face and clung there, I shuddered as one who had encountered a phantom.

I was glad enough when I reached my room and locked out the mould and the darkness. A cheery fire was burning in the grate, and I sat down before it with a comforting sense of relief. For two hours I sat there, thinking of bygone times; recalling old scenes, and summoning half-forgotten faces out of the mists of the past; listening, in fancy, to voices that long ago grew silent for all time, and to once familiar songs that nobody sings now. And as my reverie softened down to a sadder and sadder pathos, the shrieking of the winds outside softened to a wail, the angry beating of the rain against the panes diminished to a tranquil patter, and one by one the noises in the street subsided, until

the hurrying foot-steps of the last belated straggler died away in the distance and left no sound behind.

The fire had burned low. A sense of loneliness crept over me. I arose and undressed, moving on tiptoe about the room, doing stealthily what I had to do, as if I were environed by sleeping enemies whose slumbers it would be fatal to break. I covered up in bed, and lay listening to the rain and wind and the faint creaking of distant shutters, till they lulled me to sleep.

I slept profoundly, but how long I do not know. All at once I found myself awake, and filled with a shuddering expectancy. All was still. All but my own heart—I could hear it beat. Presently the bed- clothes began to slip away slowly toward the foot of the bed, as if some one were pulling them! I could not stir; I could not speak. Still the blankets slipped deliberately away, till my breast was uncovered. Then with a great effort I seized them and drew them over my head. I waited, listened, waited. Once more that steady pull began, and once more I lay torpid a century of dragging seconds till my breast was naked again. At last I roused my energies and snatched the covers back to their place and held them with a strong grip. I waited. By and by I felt a faint tug, and took a fresh grip. The tug strengthened to a steady strain—it grew stronger and stronger. My hold parted, and for the third time the blankets slid away. I groaned. An answering groan came from the foot of the bed! Beaded drops of sweat stood upon my forehead. I was more

dead than alive. Presently I heard a heavy footstep in my room—the step of an elephant, it seemed to me—it was not like anything human. But it was moving FROM me—there was relief in that. I heard it approach the door—pass out without moving bolt or lock—and wander away among the dismal corridors, straining the floors and joists till they creaked again as it passed—and then silence reigned once more.

When my excitement had calmed, I said to myself, "This is a dream—simply a hideous dream." And so I lay thinking it over until I convinced myself that it WAS a dream, and then a comforting laugh relaxed my lips and I was happy again. I got up and struck a light; and when I found that the locks and bolts were just as I had left them, another soothing laugh welled in my heart and rippled from my lips. I took my pipe and lit it, and was just sitting down before the fire, when—down went the pipe out of my nerveless fingers, the blood forsook my cheeks, and my placid breathing was cut short with a gasp! In the ashes on the hearth, side by side with my own bare footprint, was another, so vast that in comparison mine was but an infant's! Then I had HAD a visitor, and the elephant tread was explained.

I put out the light and returned to bed, palsied with fear. I lay a long time, peering into the darkness, and listening. Then I heard a grating noise overhead, like the dragging of a heavy body across the floor; then the throwing down of the body, and the shaking of my windows in response to the concussion. In distant parts of the building I heard the muffled slamming of doors. I heard, at intervals, stealthy footsteps

Ye
Ghost
Story

creeping in and out among the corridors, and up and down the stairs. Sometimes these noises approached my door, hesitated, and went away again. I heard the clanking of chains faintly, in remote passages, and listened while the clanking grew nearer—while it wearily climbed the stairways, marking each move by the loose surplus of chain that fell with an accented rattle upon each succeeding step as the goblin that bore it advanced. I heard muttered sentences; half-uttered screams that seemed smothered violently; and the swish of invisible garments, the rush of invisible wings. Then I became conscious that my chamber was invaded—that I was not alone. I heard sighs and breathings about my bed, and mysterious whisperings. Three little spheres of soft phosphorescent light appeared on the ceiling directly over my head, clung and glowed there a moment, and then dropped—two of them upon my face and one upon the pillow. They spattered, liquidly, and felt warm. Intuition told me they had turned to gouts of blood as they fell—I needed no light to satisfy myself of that. Then I saw pallid faces, dimly luminous, and white uplifted hands, floating bodiless in the air—floating a moment and then disappearing. The whispering ceased, and the voices and the sounds, and a solemn stillness followed. I waited and listened. I felt that I must have light or die. I was weak with fear. I slowly raised myself toward a sitting posture, and my face came in contact with a clammy hand! All strength went from me apparently, and I fell back

like a stricken invalid. Then I heard the rustle of a garment—it seemed to pass to the door and go out.

When everything was still once more, I crept out of bed, sick and feeble, and lit the gas with a hand that trembled as if it were aged with a hundred years. The light brought some little cheer to my spirits. I sat down and fell into a dreamy contemplation of that great footprint in the ashes. By and by its outlines began to waver and grow dim. I glanced up and the broad gas flame was slowly wilting away. In the same moment I heard that elephantine tread again. I noted its approach, nearer and nearer, along the musty halls, and dimmer and dimmer the light waned. The tread reached my very door and paused—the light had dwindled to a sickly blue, and all things about me lay in a spectral twilight. The door did not open, and yet I felt a faint gust of air fan my cheek, and presently was conscious of a huge, cloudy presence before me. I watched it with fascinated eyes. A pale glow stole over the Thing; gradually its cloudy folds took shape—an arm appeared, then legs, then a body, and last a great sad face looked out of the vapor. Stripped of its filmy housings, naked, muscular and comely, the majestic Cardiff Giant loomed above me!

All my misery vanished—for a child might know that no harm could come with that benignant countenance. My cheerful spirits returned at once, and in sympathy with them the gas flamed up brightly again. Never a lonely outcast was so glad to welcome company as I was to greet the friendly giant. I said:

"Why, is it nobody but you? Do you know, I have been scared to death for the last two or three hours? I am most honestly glad to see you. I wish I had a chair—Here, here, don't try to sit down in that thing!

But it was too late. He was in it before I could stop him, and down he went—I never saw a chair shiver so in my life.

"Stop, stop, You'll ruin ev—"

Too late again. There was another crash, and another chair was resolved into its original elements.

"Confound it, haven't you got any judgment at all? Do you want to ruin all the furniture on the place? Here, here, you petrified fool—"

But it was no use. Before I could arrest him he had sat down on the bed, and it was a melancholy ruin.

"Now what sort of a way is that to do? First you come lumbering about the place bringing a legion of vagabond goblins along with you to worry me to death, and then when I overlook an indelicacy of costume which would not be tolerated anywhere by cultivated people except in a respectable theater, and not even there if the nudity were of YOUR sex, you repay me by wrecking all the furniture you can find to sit down on. And why will you? You damage yourself as much as you do me. You have broken off the end of your spinal column, and littered up the floor with chips of your hams till the place looks like a marble yard. You ought to be ashamed of yourself—you are big enough to know better."

"Well, I will not break any more furniture. But what am I to do?

I have not had a chance to sit down for a century." And the tears came into his eyes.

"Poor devil," I said, "I should not have been so harsh with you. And you are an orphan, too, no doubt. But sit down on the floor here—nothing else can stand your weight—and besides, we cannot be sociable with you away up there above me; I want you down where I can perch on this high counting-house stool and gossip with you face to face."

So he sat down on the floor, and lit a pipe which I gave him, threw one of my red blankets over his shoulders, inverted my sitz-bath on his head, helmet fashion, and made himself picturesque and comfortable. Then he crossed his ankles, while I renewed the fire, and exposed the flat, honey-combed bottoms of his prodigious feet to the grateful warmth.

"What is the matter with the bottom of your feet and the back of your legs, that they are gouged up so?"

"Infernal chillblains—I caught them clear up to the back of my head, roosting out there under Newell's farm. But I love the place; I love it as one loves his old home. There is no peace for me like the peace I feel when I am there."

We talked along for half an hour, and then I noticed that he looked tired, and spoke of it. "Tired?" he said. "Well, I should think so. And now I will tell you all about it, since you have treated me so well. I am the spirit of the Petrified Man that lies across the street there in the Museum. I am the ghost of the Cardiff Giant. I can have no rest, no peace, till they have given that poor body burial again. Now what was the most natural thing for me to do, to make men satisfy this wish? Terrify them into it!—haunt the place where the body lay! So I haunted the museum night after night. I even got other spirits to help me. But it did no good, for nobody ever came to the museum at midnight. Then it occurred to me to come over the way and haunt this place a little. I felt that if I ever got a hearing I must succeed, for I had the most efficient company that perdition could furnish. Night after night we have shivered around through these mildewed halls, dragging chains, groaning, whispering, tramping up and down stairs, till, to tell you the truth, I am almost worn out. But when I saw a light in your room tonight I roused my energies again and went at it with a deal of the old freshness. But I am tired out—entirely fagged out. Give me, I beseech you, give me some hope!"

I lit off my perch in a burst of excitement, and exclaimed:

"This transcends everything—everything that ever did occur! Why you poor blundering old fossil, you have had all your trouble for

nothing—you have been haunting a PLASTER CAST of yourself—the real Cardiff Giant is in Albany!

Confound it, don't you know your own remains?"

I never saw such an eloquent look of shame, of pitiable humiliation, overspread a countenance before.

The Petrified Man rose slowly to his feet, and said:

"Honestly, IS that true?"

"As true as I am sitting here."

He took the pipe from his mouth and laid it on the mantel, then stood irresolute a moment (unconsciously, from old habit, thrusting his hands where his pantaloons pockets should have been, and meditatively dropping his chin on his breast), and finally said:

"Well—I NEVER felt so absurd before. The Petrified Man has sold everybody else, and now the mean fraud has ended by selling its own ghost! My son, if there is any charity left in your heart for a poor friendless phantom like me, don't let this get out. Think how YOU would feel if you had made such an ass of yourself."

I heard his stately tramp die away, step by step down the stairs and out into the deserted street, and felt sorry that he was gone, poor fellow—and sorrier still that he had carried off my red blanket and my bath tub.

WITCHES' BREW

This delicious fruity drink will give you a magical boost on those cold winter nights. While the cauldron can be substituted with a regular pot, you may find the brew loses some of its potency. For a little extra zip, add a few drops of full moon water just before serving.

3 cups apple cider
1 cup cranberry juice
1 stick cinnamon
1 teaspoon whole cloves
1 tablespoon honey

1. Put all ingredients in a small cauldron on the stove.
2. Heat well, but do not boil.
3. Strain out cloves and cinnamon stick.
4. Serve hot in mugs. (Goes very well with Gingerbread Ghosts!)

Apple Dunking

An age-old Halloween tradition, apple dunking is more than just a fun party game. Follow the rules and this custom can foretell the future! Fill up a basin with water and throw in a whole bunch of fresh red apples. Invite your friends to gather around the tub and try to bite hold of an apple WITHOUT using their arms or hands. The first one to successfully raise their head with an apple in their mouth will be the first to be married!

A Halloween Spell

Here's a special spell that very few non-magical people have ever heard about . . .

On Halloween night, catch an autumn leaf as it falls from its branch toward the ground below, and you and your family will have a year of good fortune. Let it drop and the leaf's magic will be lost forever!

NIGHT
BELL
DOCTOR
BROWN

APPEAR TO FEEL NO PAIN

Stick a pile of sharp, shiny pins into your thumb without breaking a sweat—or shedding a drop of blood.

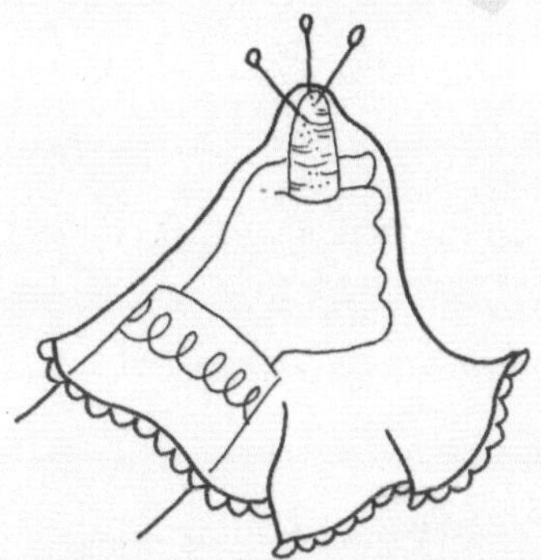

Break a carrot in half and hide half of it in your fist. Hold up your fist, with your thumb pointing up, and tell your friends that you will now stick pins into your thumb and not feel a thing.

Place a handkerchief over your fist. Slip your thumb down and put the carrot in its place as you lower the hanky.

Stick pins into the carrot, then dramatically take them out. Let the carrot fall back into your hand as you stick up your thumb.

Swoosh the handkerchief away and show everyone your unharmed, magic thumb.

THE CURSE OF THE HINEMOA

In 1892, the ship Hinemoa—named after the beautiful and graceful daughter of a very powerful New Zealand chief—set sail on a chilling journey of terror. A ghastly string of bad luck for its first captains revealed that something was terribly wrong with the steamer. The first captain went insane and had to be replaced. The next fell victim of foul play and was thrown into prison. The third man at the helm became a drunk and, shaking from DT's, lost his job. Captain number four mysteriously died in his cabin, and on the fifth voyage, the captain committed suicide.

The next time the Hinemoa went to sea, it lost its balance and overturned. Righted again, it set sail once more and put its curse on two sailors, washing them overboard into the Pacific.

The curse continued until the last voyage of the Hinemoa in September 1917. Instead of a graceful

retirement, the unfortunate vessel was unlucky enough to cross paths with an deadly German submarine. Shortly thereafter, the Hinemoa sank, bringing the curse to a watery end.

The Hinemoa's faithful crew knew why the ship was cursed: Deadly forces entered the ship while it was being built, they claimed, and were stored up in the heart of the vessel. How did they arrive, and in what material? The first ballast—heavy material used to give the ship stability—was gravel from a London graveyard.

THE MONKEY'S PAW

BY W. W. JACOBS

Without, the night was cold and wet, but in the small parlor of Lakesnam Villa the blinds were drawn and the fire burned brightly. Father and son were at chess, the former, who possessed ideas about the game involving radical changes, putting his king into such sharp and unnecessary perils that it even provoked comment from the white-haired old lady knitting placidly by the fire.

"Hark at the wind," said Mr. White, who, having seen a fatal mistake after it was too late, was amiably desirous of preventing his son from seeing it.

"I'm listening," said the latter, grimly surveying the board as he stretched out his hand. "Check."

"I should hardly think that he'd come tonight," said his father, with his hand poised over the board.

"Mate," replied the son.

"That's the worst of living so far out," bawled Mr. White, with sudden and unlooked-for violence; "of all the beastly, slushy, out-of-the-way places to live in, this is the worst. Pathway's a bog, and the road's a torrent. I don't know what people are thinking about. I suppose because only two houses on the road are let, they think it doesn't matter."

"Never mind, dear," said his wife soothingly; "perhaps you'll win the next one."

Mr. White looked up sharply, just in time to intercept a knowing glance between mother and son. The words died away on his lips, and he hid a guilty grin in his thin gray beard.

"There he is," said Herbert White, as the gate banged to loudly and heavy footsteps came toward the door.

The old man rose with hospitable haste, and opening the door, was heard condoling with the new arrival. The new arrival also condoled with himself, so that Mrs. White said, "Tut, tut!" and coughed gently as her husband entered the room, followed by a tall burly man, beady of eye and rubicund of visage.

"Sergeant Major Morris," he said, introducing him.

The sergeant major shook hands, and taking the proffered seat by the fire, watched contentedly while his host got out whisky and tumblers and stood a small copper kettle on the fire.

At the third glass his eyes got brighter, and he began to talk, the little family circle regarding with eager interest this visitor from distant parts, as he squared his broad shoulders in the chair and spoke of strange scenes and doughty deeds, of wars and plagues and strange peoples.

"Twenty-one years of it," said Mr. White, nodding at his wife and son. "When he went away he was a slip of a youth in the warehouse. Now look at him."

"He don't look to have taken much harm," said Mrs. White politely.

"I'd like to go to India myself," said the old man, "just to look round a bit, you know."

"Better where you are," said the sergeant major, shaking his head. He put down the empty glass and, sighing softly, shook it again.

"I should like to see those old temples and fakirs and jugglers," said the old man. "What was that you started telling me the other day about a monkey's paw or something, Morris?"

"Nothing," said the soldier hastily. "Leastways, nothing worth hearing."

"Monkey's paw?" said Mrs. White curiously.

"Well, it's just a bit of what you might call magic, perhaps," said the sergeant major offhandedly.

His three listeners leaned forward eagerly. The visitor absent-mindedly put his empty glass to his lips and then set it down again. His host filled it for him.

"To look at," said the sergeant major, fumbling in his pocket, "it's just an ordinary little paw, dried to a mummy."

He took something out of his pocket and proffered it. Mrs. White drew back with a grimace, but her son, taking it, examined it curiously.

"And what is there special about it?" inquired Mr. White, as he took it from his son and, having examined it, placed it upon the table.

"It had a spell put on it by an old fakir," said the sergeant major, "a very holy man. He wanted to show that fate ruled people's lives, and that those who interfered with it did so to their sorrow. He put a spell on it so that three separate men could have three wishes from it."

His manner was so impressive that his hearers were conscious that their light laughter jarred somewhat.

"Well, why don't you have three, sir?" said Herbert White cleverly.

The soldier regarded him in the way that middle age is wont to regard presumptuous youth. "I have," he said quietly, and his blotchy face whitened.

"And did you really have the three wishes granted?" asked Mrs. White.

"I did," said the sergeant major, and his glass tapped against his strong teeth.

"And has anybody else wished?" inquired the old lady.

"The first man had his three wishes, yes," was the reply. "I don't know what the first two were, but the third was for death. That's how I got the paw."

His tones were so grave that a hush fell upon the group.

"If you've had your three wishes, it's no good to you now, then, Moris," said the old man at last. "What do you keep it for?"

The soldier shook his head. "Fancy, I suppose," he said slowly. "I did have some idea of selling it, but I don't think I will. It has

caused enough mischief already. Besides, people won't buy. They think it's a fairy tale, some of them, and those who do think anything of it want to try it first and pay me afterward."

"If you could have another three wishes," said the old man, eyeing him keenly, "would you have them?"

"I don't know," said the other. "I don't know."

He took the paw, and dangling it between his front finger and thumb, suddenly threw it upon the fire. White, with a slight cry, stooped down and snatched it off.

"Better let it burn," said the soldier solemnly.

"If you don't want it, Morris," said the old man, "give it to me."

"I won't," said his friend doggedly. "I threw it on the fire. If you keep it, don't blame me for what happens. Pitch it on the fire again, like a sensible man."

The other shook his head and examined his new possession closely. "How do you do it?" he inquired.

"Hold it up in your right hand and wish aloud," said the sergeant major, "but I warn you of the consequences."

"Sounds like the *Arabian Nights*," said Mrs. White, as she rose and began to set the supper. "Don't you think you might wish for four pairs of hands for me?"

Her husband drew the talisman from his pocket and then all three burst into laughter as the sergeant major, with a look of alarm on his face, caught him by the arm.

"If you must wish," he said gruffly, "wish for something sensible."

Mr. White dropped it back into his pocket, and placing chairs, motioned his friend to the table. In the business of supper the talisman was partly forgotten, and afterward the three sat listening in an enthralled fashion to a second installment of the soldier's adventures in India.

"If the tale about the monkey's paw is not more truthful than those he has been telling us," said Herbert, as the door closed behind their guest, just in time for him to catch the last train, "we shan't make much out of it."

"Did you give him anything for it, father?" inquired Mrs. White, regarding her husband closely.

"A trifle," said he, coloring slightly. "He didn't want it, but I made him take it. And he pressed me again to throw it away."

"Likely," said Herbert, with pretended horror. "Why, we're going to be rich, and famous, and happy. Wish to be an emperor, father, to begin with; then you can't be henpecked."

He darted round the table, pursued by the maligned Mrs. White armed with an antimacassar.

Mr. White took the paw from his pocket and eyed it dubiously. "I don't know what to wish for, and that's a fact," he said slowly. "It seems to me I've got all I want."

"If you only cleared the house, you'd be quite happy, wouldn't you?" said Herbert, with his hand on his shoulder. "Well, wish for two hundred pounds, then; that'll just do it."

His father, smiling shamefacedly at his own credulity, held up the talisman, as his son, with a solemn face somewhat marred by a wink at his mother, sat down at the piano and struck a few impressive chords.

"I wish for two hundred pounds," said the old man distinctly.

A fine crash from the piano greeted the words, interrupted by a shuddering cry from the old man. His wife and son ran toward him.

"It moved," he cried, with a glance of disgust at the object as it lay on the floor. "As I wished it twisted in my hands like a snake."

"Well, I don't see the money," said his son, as he picked it up and placed it on the table, "and I bet I never shall."

"It must have been your fancy, father," said his wife, regarding him anxiously.

He shook his head. "Never mind, though; there's no harm done, but it gave me a shock all the same."

They sat down by the fire again while the two men finished their pipes. Outside, the wind was higher than ever, and the old man started nervously at the sound of a door banging upstairs. A silence unusual and depressing settled upon all three, which lasted until the old couple rose to retire for the night.

"I expect you'll find the cash tied up in a big bag in the middle of your bed," said Herbert, as he bade them good night, "and something horrible squatting up on top of the wardrobe watching you as you pocket your ill-gotten gains."

II.

In the brightness of the wintry sun next morning as it streamed over the breakfast table, Herbert laughed at his fears. There was an air of prosaic wholesomeness about the room which it had lacked on the previous night, and the dirty, shriveled little paw was pitched on the sideboard with a carelessness which betokened no great belief in its virtues.

"I suppose all old soldiers are the same," said Mrs. White. "The idea of our listening to such nonsense! How could wishes be granted in these days? And if they could, how could two hundred pounds hurt you, father?"

"Might drop on his head from the sky," said the frivolous Herbert.

"Morris said the things happened so naturally," said his father, "that you might if you so wished attribute it to coincidence."

"Well, don't break into the money before I come back," said Herbert, as he rose from the table. "I'm afraid it'll turn you into a mean, avaricious man, and we shall have to disown you."

His mother laughed, and following him to the door, watched him down the road, and returning to the breakfast table, was very happy at the expense of her husband's credulity. All of which did not prevent her from scurrying to the door at the postman's knock, nor prevent her from referring somewhat shortly to retired sergeant majors of bibulous habits when she found that the post brought a tailor's bill.

"Herbert will have some more of his funny remarks, I expect, when he comes home," she said, as they sat at dinner.

"I dare say," said Mr. White, pouring himself out some beer; "but for all that, the thing moved in my hand; that I'll swear to."

"You thought it did," said the old lady soothingly.

"I say it did," replied the other. "There was no thought about it; I had just—What's the matter?"

His wife made no reply. She was watching the mysterious movements of a man outside, who, peering in an undecided fashion at the house, appeared to be trying to make up his mind to enter. In mental connection with the two hundred pounds, she noticed that the stranger was well-dressed and wore a silk hat of glossy newness. Three times he paused at the gate, and then walked on again. The fourth time he stood with his hand upon it, and then with sudden resolution flung it open and walked up the path. Mrs. White at the same moment placed her hands behind her, and hurriedly unfastening the strings of her apron, put that useful article of apparel beneath the cushion of her chair.

She brought the stranger, who seemed ill at ease, into the room. He gazed furtively at Mrs. White, and listened in a preoccupied fashion as the old lady apologized for the appearance of the room, and her husband's coat, a garment which he usually reserved for the garden. She

then waited as patiently as her sex would permit for him to broach his business, but he was at first strangely silent.

"I—was asked to call," he said at last, and stooped and picked a piece of cotton from his trousers. "I come from Maw and Meggins."

The old lady started. "Is anything the matter?" she asked breathlessly. "Has anything happened to Herbert? What is it? What is it?"

Her husband interposed. "There, there, mother," he said hastily. "Sit down, and don't jump to conclusions. You've not brought bad news, I'm sure, sir," and he eyed the other wistfully.

"I'm sorry—" began the visitor.

"Is he hurt?" demanded the mother.

The visitor bowed in assent. "Badly hurt," he said quietly, "but he is not in any pain."

"Oh, thank God!" said the old woman, clasping her hands. "Thank God for that! Thank—"

She broke off suddenly as the sinister meaning of the assurance dawned upon her and she saw the awful confirmation of her fears in the other's averted face. She caught her breath, and turning to her slower-witted husband, laid her trembling old hand upon his. There was a long silence.

"He was caught in the machinery," said the visitor at length, in a low voice.

"Caught in the machinery," repeated Mr. White, in a dazed fashion, "yes."

He sat staring blankly out at the window, and taking his wife's hand between his own, pressed it as he had been wont to do in their old courting days nearly forty years before.

"He was the only one left us," he said, turning gently to the visitor. "It is hard."

The other coughed, and rising, walked slowly to the window. "The firm wished me to convey their sincere sympathy with you in your great loss," he said, without looking round. "I beg that you will understand I am only their servant and merely obeying orders."

There was no reply; the old woman's face was white, her eyes staring, and her breath inaudible; on the husband's face was a look such as his friend the sergeant might have carried into his first action.

"I was to say that Maw and Meggins disclaim all responsibility," continued the other. "They admit no liability at all, but in consideration of your son's services they wish to present you with a certain sum as compensation."

Mr. White dropped his wife's hand, and rising to his feet, gazed with a look of horror at his visitor. His dry lips shaped the words, "How much?"

"Two hundred pounds," was the answer.

Unconscious of his wife's shriek, the old man smiled faintly, put out his hands like a sightless man, and dropped, a senseless heap, to the floor.

III.

In the huge new cemetery, some two miles distant, the old people buried their dead, and came back to a house steeped in shadow and silence. It was all over so quickly that at first they could hardly realize it, and remained in a state of expectation as though of something else to happen—something else which was to lighten this load, too heavy for old hearts to bear. But the days passed, and expectation gave place to resignation—the hopeless resignation of the old, sometimes miscalled apathy. Sometimes they hardly exchanged a word, for now they had nothing to talk about, and their days were long to weariness.

It was about a week after that that the old man, waking suddenly in the night, stretched out his hand and found himself alone. The room was in darkness, and the sound of subdued weeping came from the window. He raised himself in bed and listened.

"Come back," he said tenderly. "You will be cold."

"It is colder for my son," said the old woman, and wept afresh.

The sound of her sobs died away on his ears. The bed was warm, and his eyes heavy with sleep. He dozed fitfully, and then slept until a sudden wild cry from his wife awoke him with a start.

"The monkey's paw!" she cried wildly. "The monkey's paw!"

He started up in alarm. "Where? Where is it? What's the matter?"

She came stumbling across the room toward him. "I want it," she said quietly. "You've not destroyed it?"

"It's in the parlor, on the bracket," he replied, marveling. "Why?"

She cried and laughed together, and bending over, kissed his cheek.

"I only just thought of it," she said hysterically. "Why didn't I think of it before? Why didn't you think of it?"

"Think of what?" he questioned.

"The other two wishes," she replied rapidly. "We've only had one."

"Was not that enough?" he demanded fiercely.

"No," she cried triumphantly; "we'll have one more. Go down and get it quickly, and wish our boy alive again."

The man sat up in bed and flung the bedclothes from his quaking limbs. "Good God, you are mad!" he cried, aghast.

"Get it," she panted; "get it quickly, and wish—Oh, my boy, my boy!"

Her husband struck a match and lit the candle. "Get back to bed," he said unsteadily. "You don't know what you are saying."

"We had the first wish granted," said the old woman feverishly; "why not the second?"

"A coincidence," stammered the old man.

"Go and get it and wish," cried the old woman, and dragged him toward the door.

He went down in the darkness, and felt his way to the parlor, and then to the mantelpiece. The talisman was in its place, and a horrible fear that the unspoken wish might bring his mutilated son before him ere he could escape from the room seized upon him, and he caught his

breath as he found that he had lost the direction of the door. His brow cold with sweat, he felt his way round the table, and groped along the wall until he found himself in the small passage with the unwholesome thing in his hand.

Even his wife's face seemed changed as he entered the room. It was white and expectant, and to his fears seemed to have an unusual look upon it. He was afraid of her.

"Wish!" she cried, in a strong voice.

"It is foolish and wicked," he faltered.

"Wish!" repeated his wife.

He raised his hand. "I wish my son alive again."

The talisman fell to the floor, and he regarded it shudderingly. Then he sank trembling into a chair as the old woman, with burning eyes, walked to the window and raised the blind.

He sat until he was chilled with the cold, glancing occasionally at the figure of the old woman peering through the window. The candle end, which had burnt below the rim of the china candlestick, was throwing pulsating shadows on the ceiling and walls, until, with a flicker larger than the rest, it expired. The old man, with an unspeakable sense of relief at the failure of the talisman, crept back to his bed, and a minute or two afterward the old woman came silently and apathetically beside him.

Neither spoke, but both lay silently listening to the ticking of the clock. A stair creaked, and a squeaky mouse scurried noisily through the wall. The darkness was oppressive, and after lying for some time screwing up his courage, the husband took the box of matches, and striking one, went downstairs for a candle.

At the foot of the stairs the match went out, and he paused to strike another, and at the same moment a knock, so quiet and stealthy as to be scarcely audible, sounded on the front door.

The matches fell from his hand. He stood motionless, his breath suspended until the knock was repeated. Then he turned and fled swiftly back to his room, and closed the door behind him. A third knock sounded through the house.

"What's that?" cried the old woman, starting up.

"A rat," said the old man, in shaking tones— "a rat. it passed me on the stairs."

His wife sat up in bed, listening. A loud knock resounded through the house.

"It's Herbert!" she screamed. "It's Herbert!"

She ran to the door, but her husband was before her, and catching her by the arm, held her tightly.

"What are you going to do?" he whispered hoarsely.

"It's my boy; it's Herbert!" she cried, struggling mechanically. "I forgot it was two miles away. What are you holding me for? Let go. I must open the door."

"For God's sake don't let it in," cried the old man, trembling.

"You're afraid of your own son," she cried, struggling. "Let me go. I'm coming, Herbert; I'm coming."

There was another knock, and another. The old woman with a sudden wrench broke free and ran from the room. Her husband followed to the landing, and called after her appealingly as she hurried downstairs. He heard the chain rattle back and the bottom bolt drawn slowly and stiffly from the socket. Then the old woman's voice, strained and panting.

"The bolt," she cried loudly. "Come down. I can't reach it."

But her husband was on his hands and knees groping wildly on the floor in search of the paw. If he could only find it before the thing outside got in. A perfect fusillade of knocks reverberated through the house, and he heard the scraping of a chair as his wife put it down in the passage against the door. He heard the creaking of the bolt as it came slowly back, and at the same moment, he found the monkey's paw, and frantically breathed his third and last wish.

The knocking ceased suddenly, although the echoes of it were still in the house. He heard the chair drawn back and the door opened. A cold wind rushed up the staircase, and a long loud wail of disappointment and misery from his wife gave him courage to run down to her side, and then to the gate beyond. The street lamp flickering opposite shone on a quiet and deserted road.

The Raven

by Edgar Allan Poe

Once upon a midnight dreary, while I pondered, weak and weary,
Over many a quaint and curious volume of forgotten lore—
While I nodded, nearly napping, suddenly there came a tapping,
As of some one gently rapping, rapping at my chamber door.
"'Tis some visitor," I muttered, tapping at my chamber door—
Only this and nothing more."

Ah, distinctly I remember it was in the bleak December,
And each separate dying ember wrought its ghost upon the floor.
Eagerly I wished the morrow;—vainly I had sought to borrow
From my books surcease of sorrow—sorrow for the lost Lenore—
For the rare and radiant maiden whom the angels name Lenore—
Nameless here for evermore.

Open here I flung the shutter, when, with many a flirt and flutter,
In there stepped a stately Raven of the saintly days of yore.
Not the least obeisance made he; not a minute stopped or stayed he,
But, with mien of lord or lady, perched above my chamber door—
Perched upon a bust of Pallas just above my chamber door—
Perched, and sat, and nothing more.

Then this ebony bird beguiling my sad fancy into smiling,
By the grave and stern decorum of the countenance it wore,
"Though thy crest be shorn and shaven, thou," I said, "art sure no craven,
Ghastly grim and ancient Raven wandering from the Nightly shore—
Tell me what thy lordly name is on the Night's Plutonian shore!"
Quoth the Raven, "Nevermore."

Much I marvelled this ungainly fowl to hear discourse so plainly,
Though its answer little meaning—little relevancy bore;
For we cannot help agreeing that no living human being
Ever yet was blessed with seeing bird above his chamber door—
Bird or beast upon the sculptured bust above his chamber door,
With such name as "Nevermore."

But the Raven, sitting lonely on that placid bust, spoke only
That one word, as if his soul in that one word he did outpour.
Nothing farther then he uttered; not a feather then he fluttered—
Till I scarcely more than muttered: "Other friends have flown before—
On the morrow *he* will leave me as my Hopes have flown before."
Then the bird said, "Nevermore."

Startled at the stillness broken by reply so aptly spoken,
"Doubtless," said I, "what it utters is its only stock and store,
Caught from some unhappy master whom unmerciful Disaster

Followed fast and followed faster till his songs one burden bore—
Till the dirges of his Hope that melancholy burden bore
        Of 'Never—nevermore.'"

But the Raven still beguiling all my sad soul into smiling,
Straight I wheeled a cushioned seat in front of bird and bust and door;
Then, upon the velvet sinking, I betook myself to linking
Fancy unto fancy, thinking what this ominous bird of yore—
What this grim, ungainly, ghastly, gaunt, and ominous bird of your
        Meant in croaking "Nevermore."

Be that word our sign of parting, bird or fiend!" I shrieked, upstarting—
"Get thee back into the tempest and the Night's Plutonian shore!
Leave no black plume as a token of that lie thy soul hath spoken!
Leave my loneliness unbroken!—quit the bust above my door!
Take thy beak from out my heart, and take thy form from off my door!"
        Quoth the Raven, "Nevermore."

And the Raven, never flitting, still is sitting, still is sitting
On the pallid bust of Pallas just above my chamber door;
And his eyes have all the seeming of a demon's that is dreaming,
And the lamp-light o'er him streaming throws his shadow on the floor;
And my soul from out that shadow that lies floating on the floor
        Shall be lifted—nevermore!

BAKED APPLES

6 medium-sized apples
1/4 cup granulated sugar
1/2 cup brown sugar
6 tablespoons butter
3 teaspoons ground cinnamon

1. Preheat oven to 350°F.
2. In a small bowl, mix together brown and granulated sugars. Add butter and cream together.
3. Core apples, but do not cut all the way through. Place them in a baking dish filled with half an inch of water.
4. Fill each apple with three table spoons of sugar and butter mixture.
5. Sprinkle 1/2 teaspoon of cinnamon on top of each apple.
6. Bake 15 -20 minutes or until apples are tender.
7. Serve warm with vanilla ice cream.

Serves six

The Story of the Jack-o'-Lantern

A long time ago an Irishman named Jack found himself face to face with the Devil while sipping whiskey at a local pub. Satan had come to claim Jack's soul. But Jack, a con artist to the core, tricked the Devil into climbing a nearby tree on a dare. No sooner had the Dark Prince triumphantly reached the top branch, when Jack quickly pulled out a knife and carved a crucifix into the trunk, trapping the Devil in the tree.

Jack escaped that night with his soul intact, but continued to live out the rest of his days as a trickster and a drunk. When he died at a ripe old age, Jack was turned away from Heaven's gates for living such a dishonest and sinful life. So arriving at Hell's flaming threshold, Jack found himself staring into Satan's eyes once again. The devil fixed him with an evil glare and refused him entry into the fiery pit. Stranded in the blackness between Heaven and Hell, Jack begged the Devil for a candle to light his way. The Devil threw him a burning coal and turned his back on Jack forever. Jack placed the ember in a carved out turnip, using it as a lantern as he wandered the netherworlds in anguish.

The Jack-o'-Lantern soon became the Irish symbol for a damned soul and was often placed in a window on Halloween to scare off evil spirits. When the Irish later immigrated to America, they began using pumpkins to make these superstitious lanterns instead of turnips, which were less plentiful and harder to come by. Today, Jack-o'-Lanterns are a favorite Halloween tradition, used as spooky decorations rather than spiritual watchmen.

The Abracadaba Spell

Abracadabra! This word might be the most famous magical utterance in the world. But did you know that it was originally used in a spell against fever and illness? To perform the authentic Abracadabra spell, write the letters A-B-R-A-C-A-D-A-B-R-A on a small piece of paper as shown in following diagram:

A B R A C A D A B A R A
A B R A C A D A B R
A B R A C A D A B
A B R A C A D A
A B R A C A D
A B R A C A
A B R A C
A B R A
A B R
A B
A

Thread a piece of string or ribbon through the paper and hang it around the neck of the feverish patient. Just as the letters of the word ABRACADABRA disappear, so should person's illness.

Test your natural talent in the magical healing arts by trying this spell out on a brother or sister who is sick with the flu.

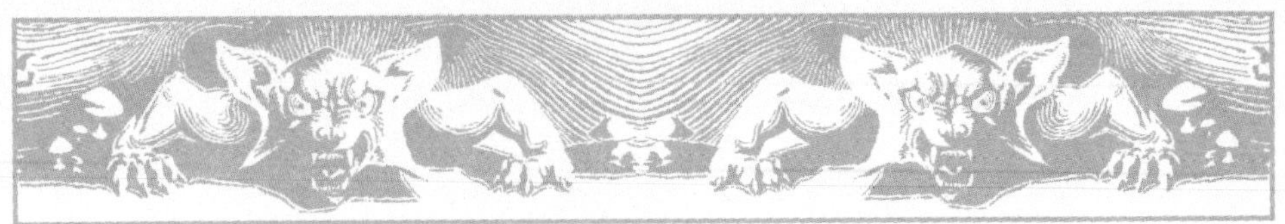

The Foundling

by Lloyd Alexander

This is told of Dallben, greatest of enchanters in Prydain: how three black-robed hags found him, when he was still a baby, in a basket at the edge of the Marshes of Morva. "Oh, Orddu, see what's here!" cried the one named Orwen, peering into the wicker vessel floating amid the tall grasses. "Poor lost duckling! He'll catch his death of cold! Whatever shall we do with him?"

"A sweet morsel," croaked the one named Orgoch from the depths of her hood. "A tender lamb. I know what I should do."

"Please be silent, Orgoch," said the one named Orddu. "You've already had your breakfast." Orddu was a short, plump woman with a round, lumpy face and sharp black eyes. Jewels, pins, and brooches glittered in her tangle of weedy hair. "We can't leave him here to get all soggy. I suppose we shall have to take him home with us."

"Oh, yes!" exclaimed Orwen, dangling her string of milky white beads over the tiny figure in the basket. "Ah, the darling tadpole! Look at his pink cheeks and chubby little fingers! He's smiling at us, Orddu! He's waving! But what shall we call him? He mustn't go bare and nameless."

"If you ask me—" began Orgoch.

"No one did," replied Orddu. "You are quite right, Orwen. We must give him a name. Otherwise, how shall we know who he is?"

"We have so many names lying around the cottage," said Orwen. "Some of them never used. Give him a nice, fresh, unwrinkled one."

"There's a charming name I'd been saving for special occasion," Orddu said, "but I can't remember what I did with it. No matter. His name—his name: Dallben."

"Lovely!" cried Orwen, clapping her hands. "Oh, Orddu, you have such good taste."

"Taste, indeed!" snorted Orgoch. "Dallben? Why call him Dallben?"

"Why not?" returned Orddu. "It will do splendidly. Very good quality, very durable. It should last him a lifetime."

"It will last him," Orgoch muttered, "as long as he needs it."

And so Dallben was named and nursed by these three, and given a home in their cottage near the Marshes of Morva. Under their care he grew sturdy, bright, and fair of face. He was kind and generous, and each day handsomer and happier.

The hags did not keep from him that he was a foundling. But when he was of an age to wonder about such matters, he asked where indeed he had come from, and what the rest of the world was like.

"My dear chicken," replied Orddu, "as to where you came from, we haven't the slightest notion. Nor, might I say, the least interest. You're here with us now, to our delight, and that's quite enough to know."

"As to the rest of the world," Orwen added, "don't bother your pretty, curly head about it. You can be sure it doesn't bother about you. Be glad you were found instead of drowned. Why, this very moment you might be part of a school of fish. And what a slippery, scaly sort of life that would be."

"I like fish," muttered Orgoch, "especially eels."

"Do hush, dear Orgoch," said Orddu. "You're always thinking of your stomach."

Despite his curiosity, Dallben saw there was no use in questioning further. Cheerful and willing, he went about every task with eagerness and good grace. He drew pails of water from the well, kept the fire burning in the hearth, pumped the bellows, swept away the ashes, and dug the garden. No toil was too troublesome for him. When Orddu spun thread, he turned the spinning wheel. He helped Orwen measure the skeins into lengths and held them for Orgoch to snip with a pair of rusty shears.

One day, when the three brewed a potion of roots and herbs, Dallben was left alone to stir the huge, steaming kettle with a long iron spoon. He obeyed the hags' warning not to taste the liquid, but soon the potion began boiling so briskly that a few drops bubbled up and by

accident splashed his fingers. With a cry of pain, Dallben let fall the spoon and popped his fingers into his mouth.

His outcry brought Orddu, Orwen, and Orgoch hurrying back to the cottage.

"Oh, the poor sparrow!" gasped Orwen, seeing the boy sucking at his blistered knuckles. "He's gone and burned himself. I'll fetch an ointment for the sweet fledgling, and some spiderwebs to bandage him. What did you do with all those spiders, Orgoch? They were here only yesterday."

"Too late for all that," growled Orgoch. "Worse damage is done."

"Yes, I'm afraid so," Orddu sighed. "There's no learning without pain. The dear gosling has had his pain; and now, I daresay, he has some learning to go along with it."

Dallben, meanwhile, had swallowed the drops of liquid scalding his fingers. He licked his lips at the taste, sweet and bitter at the same time. And in that instant he began to shake with fear and excitement. All that had been common and familiar in the cottage he saw as he had never seen before.

Now he understood that the leather bellows lying by the hearth commanded the four winds; the pail of water in the corner, the

seas and oceans of the world. The earthen floor of the cottage held the roots of all plants and trees. The fire showed him the secrets of its flame, and how all things come to ashes. He gazed awe-struck at the enchantresses, for such they were.

"The threads you spin, and measure, and cut off," Dallben murmured, "these are no threads, but the lives of men. I know who you truly are."

"Oh, I doubt it," Orddu cheerfully answered. "Even we aren't always sure of that. Nevertheless, one taste of that magical brew and you know as much as we do. Almost as much, at any rate."

"Too much for his own good," muttered Orgoch.

"But what shall we do?" moaned Orwen. "He was such a sweet, innocent little robin. If only he hadn't swallowed the potion! Is there no way to make him unswallow it?"

"We could try," said Orgoch.

"No," declared Orddu. "What's done is done. You know that as well as I. Alas, the dear duckling will have to leave us. There's nothing else for it. So many people, knowing so much, under the same roof? All that knowledge crammed in, crowded, bumping and jostling back and forth? We'd not have room to breathe!"

"I say he should be kept," growled Orgoch.

"I don't think he'd like your way of keeping him," Orddu answered. She turned to Dallben. "No, my poor chicken, we must say farewell. You asked us once about the world? I'm afraid you'll have to

see it for yourself."

"But, Orddu," protested Orwen, "we can't let him march off just like that. Surely we have some little trinket he'd enjoy? A going-away present, so he won't forget us?"

"I could give him something to remember us by," began Orgoch.

"No doubt," said Orddu. "But that's not what Orwen had in mind. Of course, we shall offer him a gift. Better yet, he shall choose one for himself."

As Dallben watched, the enchantress unlocked an iron-bound chest and rummaged inside, flinging out all sorts of oddments until there was a large heap on the floor.

"Here's something," Orddu at last exclaimed. "Just the thing for a bold young chicken. A sword!"

Dallben caught his breath in wonder as Orddu put the weapon in his hands. The hilt, studded with jewels, glittered so brightly that he was dazzled and nearly blinded. The blade flashed, and a thread of fire ran along its edges.

"Take this, my duckling," Orddu said, "and you shall be the greatest warrior in Prydain. Strength and power, dear gosling! When you command, all must obey even your slightest whim."

"It is a fine blade," Dallben replied, "and comes easily to my hand."

"It shall be yours," Orddu said. "At least, as long as you're able to keep it. Oh, yes," the enchantress went on, "I should mention it's already had a number of owners. Somehow, sooner or later, it wanders back to

us. The difficulty, you see, isn't so much getting power as holding on to it. Because so many others want it, too. You'd be astonished, the lengths to which some will go. Be warned, the sword can be lost or stolen. Or bent out of shape—as, indeed, so can you, in a manner of speaking."

"And remember," put in Orwen, "you must never let it out of your sight, not for an instant."

Dallben hesitated a moment, then shook his head. "I think your gift is more burden than blessing."

"In that case," Orddu said, "perhaps this will suit you better."

As Dallben laid down the sword, the enchantress handed him a golden harp, so perfectly wrought that he no sooner held it than it seemed to play of itself.

"Take this, my sparrow," said Orddu, "and be the greatest bard in the Prydain, known throughout the land for the beauty of your songs."

Dallben's heart leaped as the instrument thrilled in his arms. He touched the sweeping curve of the glowing harp and ran his fingers over the golden strings. "I have never heard such music," he murmured. "Who owns this will surely have no lack of fame."

"You'll have fame and admiration a-plenty," said Orddu, "as long as anyone remembers you."

"Alas, that's true," Orwen said with a sigh. "Memory can be so

skimpy. It doesn't stretch very far; and, next thing you know, there's your fame gone all crumbly and mildewed."

Sadly, Dallben set down the harp. "Beautiful it is," he said, "but in the end, I fear, little help to me."

"There's nothing else we can offer at the moment," said Orddu, delving once more into the chest, "unless you'd care to have this book."

The enchantress held up a large, heavy tome and blew away the dust and cobwebs from its moldering leather binding. "It's a bulky thing for a young lamb to carry. Naturally, it would be rather weighty, for it holds everything that was ever known, is known, and will be known."

"It's full of wisdom, thick as oatmeal," added Orwen. "Quite scarce in the world—wisdom, not oatmeal—but that only makes it the more valuable."

"We have so many requests for other items," Orddu said. "Seven-league boots, cloaks of invisibility, and such great nonsense. For wisdom, practically none. Yet whoever owns this book shall have all that and more, if he likes. For the odd thing about wisdom is the more you use it the more it grows; and the more you share, the more you gain. You'd be amazed how few understand that. If they did, I suppose, they wouldn't need the book in the first place."

"Do you give this to me?" Dallben asked. "A treasure greater than all treasures?"

Orddu hesitated. "Give? Only in a manner of speaking. If you

know us as well as you say you do, then you also know we don't exactly give anything. Put it this way: We shall let you take that heavy, dusty old book if that's what you truly want. Again, be warned: The greater the treasure, the greater the cost. Nothing is given for nothing; not in the Marshes of Morva—or anyplace else, for the matter of that."

"Even so," Dallben replied, "this book is my choice."

"Very well," said Orddu, putting the ancient volume in his hands. "Now you shall be on your way. We're sorry to see you go, though sorrow is something we don't usually feel. Fare well, dear chicken. We mean this in the polite sense, for whether you fare well or ill is entirely up to you."

So Dallben took his leave of the enchantresses and set off eagerly, curious to see what lay in store not only in the world but between the covers of the book. Once the cottage was well out of sight and the marshes far behind him, he curbed his impatience no longer, but sat down by the roadside, opened the heavy tome, and began to read.

As he scanned the first pages, his eyes widened and his heart quickened. For here was knowledge he had never dreamed of: the pathways of the stars, the rounds of the planets, the ebb and flow of time and tide. All secrets of the world and all its hidden lore unfolded to him.

Dallben's head spun, giddy with delight. The huge book seemed to weigh less than a feather, and he felt so lighthearted he could have skipped from one mountaintop to the next and never touched the

ground. He laughed and sang at the top of his voice, bursting with gladness, pride, and strength in what he had learned.

"I chose well!" he cried, jumping to his feet. "But why should Orddu have warned me? Cost? What cost can there be? Knowledge is joy!"

He strode on, reading as he went. Each page lightened and sped his journey, and soon he came to a village where the dwellers danced and sang and made holiday. They offered him meat and drink and shelter for the coming night.

But Dallben thanked them for their hospitality and shook his head, saying he had meat and drink enough in the book he carried. By this time he had walked many miles, but his spirit was fresh and his legs unweary.

He kept on his way, hardly able to contain his happiness as he read and resolving not to rest until he had come to the end of the book. But he had finished less than half when the pages, to his horror, began to grow dark and stained with blood and tears.

For now the book told him of other ways of the world; of cruelty, suffering, and death. He read of greed, hatred, and war; of men striving against one another with fire and sword; of the blossoming earth trampled underfoot, of harvests lost and lives cut short. And the book told that even in the same village he had passed, a day would come when

no house would stand; when women would weep for their men, and children for their parents; and where they had offered him meat and drink, they would starve for lack of a crust of bread.

Each page he read pierced his heart. The book, which had seemed to weigh so little, now grew so heavy that his pace faltered and he staggered under the burden. Tears blinded his eyes, and he stumbled to the ground.

All night he lay shattered by despair. At dawn he stirred and found it took all his efforts even to lift his head. Bones aching, throat parched, he crept on hands and knees to quench his thirst from a puddle of water. There, at the sight of his reflection, he drew back and cried out in anguish.

His fair, bright curls had gone frost-white and fell below his brittle shoulders. His cheeks, once full and flushed with youth, were now hollow and wrinkled, half hidden by a long, gray beard. His brow, smooth yesterday, was scarred and furrowed, his hands gnarled and knotted, his eyes pale as if their color had been wept away.

Dallben bowed his head. "Yes, Orddu," he whispered, "I should have heeded you. Nothing is given without cost. But is the cost of wisdom so high? I thought knowledge was joy. Instead, it is grief beyond bearing."

The book lay nearby. Its last pages were still unread and, for a moment, Dallben thought to tear them to shreds and scatter them to the wind. Then he said:

"I have begun it, and I will finish it, whatever else it may foretell."

Fearfully and reluctantly, he began to read once more. But now his heart lifted. These pages told not only of death, but of birth as well; how the earth turns in its own time and in its own way gives back what is given to it; how things lost may be found again; and how one day ends for another to begin. He learned that the lives of men are short and filled with pain, yet each one a priceless treasure, whether it be that of a prince or a pig-keeper. And, at the last, the book taught him that while nothing was certain, all was possible.

"At the end of knowledge, wisdom begins," Dallben murmured. "And at the end of wisdom there is not grief, but hope."

He climbed to his withered legs and hobbled along his way, clasping the heavy book. After a time a farmer drove by in a horse-drawn cart, and called out to him:

"Come, Grandfather, ride with me if you like. That book must be a terrible load for an old man like you."

"Thank you just the same," Dallben answered, "but I have strength enough now to go to the end of my road."

"And where might that be?"

"I do not know," Dallben said. "I go seeking it."

ROASTED PUMPKIN SEEDS

Instead of throwing away those slippery pumpkin seeds when you carve your jack-o-lantern, put them aside and roast them later for a tasty Halloween treat.

1 1/2 cups pumpkin seeds
2 tablespoons of butter
Salt to taste

1. Preheat oven to 300°F.
2. Scoop out seeds from a fresh pumpkin. Wash seeds under cold water, removing any stringy fibers. Blot dry with paper towels and set aside in a bowl.
3. Melt butter in a saucepan and pour over the bowl of seeds. Sprinkle with salt to taste and mix until the seeds are well coated.
4. Spread the pumpkin seeds evenly in a single layer on a baking sheet. Bake for approximately 45 minutes, stirring occasionally, until seeds are golden brown.

THE CURSE OF
THE SCREAMING SKULL

Found in the town of Bettiscombe, snuggled in the heart of the English countryside, is the famous and terrifying legend of the screaming skull.

The story goes that during the 17th century a resident of Bettiscombe, Azariah Pinney, returned home after living abroad in the West Indies for some years. Azariah brought with him a slave to help care for his house and property, known as Bettiscombe Manor. The slave, however, soon fell ill and, lying upon his deathbed, made a last desperate request to his master. He asked that his corpse be sent home and buried in the land of his birth. Azariah agreed. But as soon as the slave had passed, Azariah broke his promise and buried the slave in a nearby churchyard cemetery.

The gravedigger had no sooner shoveled the last pile of dirt onto the casket, when a strange moaning drifted up through the fresh

earth. Before long, the moaning turned into an endless agonizing scream, which tore through the quiet countryside like a nightmare. The local villagers demanded that Azariah dig up the body and remove it from the cemetery immediately. So the slave was returned to Bettiscombe Manor, where Azariah stored the body in the attic. There the tortured screams ceased. The corpse remained in Azariah's home, where it decayed over time, until all that remained was the skull.

As the years passed, Bettiscombe Manor saw many owners come and go. Some did not take well to sleeping so near the infamous screaming skull and made the mistake of removing it from its resting place. One owner threw the skull into a nearby pond one stormy summer night, thinking it would sink to a watery grave. But the skull rose to the surface shrieking in anguish. Another family buried the offensive fossil in the backyard garden, but it quickly dug itself out of the ground. Ultimately, the skull was returned to the house, where it resides peacefully to this day.

The Black Cat

The black cat is the most commonly thought enchanted animal of the mystical world. Everyone knows that when a black cat crosses your path, bad luck is soon to follow. But did you know that you could counteract this evil omen with a few simple tricks? As soon as you spot the feline, spit on the ground, turn yourself around three times, or walk backward retracing your steps. For extra insurance, try reciting the following incantation:

Black Cat, I do pray,
Bring me luck and bless my way
Do not choose to bring me harm
Let me pass with this small charm

As you pass, reach down and stroke the cat's back, as a gesture of kindness.

Often the companions of witches, black cats are believed to have the power to reason, perform sorcery, and understand human languages. Many members of the magical order believe the Devil takes the form of the shadowy feline when he goes about his dark business. So the next time a black cat crosses your path, beware! It just may be the Devil in disguise . . .

A FLYING EGG

With a puff of breath, you can send an egg flying out of one glass and into another.

The secret of this trick is to use a hollow, lightweight egg. To prepare the egg, puncture a tiny hole on each end with a needle. Stick the needle deep into one of the holes and move it around to break up the yoke. Standing over a bowl or the sink, put your mouth over one of the holes and blow. Keep blowing, forcefully, until the egg has completely drained out the opposite hole. Then hold the egg under running water to rinse it out.

Place two short glasses side by side, and put the egg into one of them. Handle the egg as if its heavier than it really is. Stand close to the glass holding the egg and blow along the inside wall, next to the egg. The egg will jump out and land into the other glass.

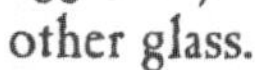

Down the Rabbit-hole

by Lewis Carroll

Alice was beginning to get very tired of sitting by her sister on the bank and of having nothing to do: once or twice she had peeped into the book her sister was reading, but it had no pictures or conversations in it, "and what is the use of a book," thought Alice, "without pictures or conversations?"

So she was considering, in her own mind (as well as she could, for the hot day made her feel very sleepy and stupid), whether the pleasure of making a daisy-chain would be worth the trouble of getting up and picking the daisies, when suddenly a White Rabbit with pink eyes ran close by her.

There was nothing so very remarkable in that; nor did Alice think it so very much out of the way to hear the Rabbit say to itself "Oh dear! Oh dear! I shall be too late!" (when she thought it over afterwards it occurred to her that she ought to have wondered at this, but at the time it all seemed quite natural); but, when the Rabbit actually *took a watch out of its waistcoat-pocket*, and looked at it, and then hurried on, Alice started to her feet, for it flashed across her mind that she had never before seen a rabbit with either a waistcoat-pocket, or a watch to take out of it, and burning with curiosity, she ran across

the field after it, and was just in time to see it pop down a large rabbit-hole under the hedge.

In another moment down went Alice after it, never once considering how in the world she was to get out again.

The rabbit-hole went straight on like a tunnel for some way, and then dipped suddenly down, so suddenly that Alice had not a moment to think about stopping herself before she found herself falling down what seemed to be a very deep well.

Either the well was very deep, or she fell very slowly, for she had plenty of time as she went down to look about her, and to wonder what was going to happen next. First, she tried to look down and make out what she was coming to, but it was too dark to see anything: then she looked at the sides of the well, and noticed that they were filled with cupboards and book-shelves: here and there she saw maps and pictures hung upon pegs. She took down a jar from one of the shelves as she passed: it was labeled "ORANGE MARMALADE," but to her great disappointment it was empty: she did not like to drop the jar, for fear of killing somebody underneath, so managed to put it into one of the cupboards as she fell past it.

"Well!" thought Alice to herself. "After such a fall as this, I shall think nothing of tumbling down-stairs! How brave they'll all

think me at home! Why, I wouldn't say anything about it, even if I fell off the top of the house!" (Which was very likely true.)

Down, down, down. Would the fall never come to an end? "I wonder how many miles I've fallen by this time?" she said aloud. "I must be getting somewhere near the centre of the earth. Let me see: that would be four thousand miles down, I think—" (for, you see, Alice had learnt several things of this sort in her lessons in the school-room, and though this was not a very good opportunity for showing off her knowledge, as there was no one to listen to her, still it was good practice to say it over) "—yes, that's about the right distance—but then I wonder what Latitude or Longitude I've got to?" (Alice had not the slightest idea what Latitude was, or Longitude either, but she thought they were nice grand words to say.)

Presently she began again. "I wonder if I shall fall right *through* the earth! How funny it'll see to come out among the people that walk with their heads downwards! The antipathies, I think—" (she was rather glad there *was* no one listening, this time, as it didn't sound at all the right word) "—but I shall have to ask them what the name of the country is, you know. Please, Ma'am, is this New Zealand? Or Australia?" (and she tried to curtsey as she spoke—fancy, curtseying as you're falling through the air! Do you think you could manage it?) "And what an ignorant little girl she'll think me for ask-

ing! No, it'll never do to ask: perhaps I shall see it written up somewhere."

Down, down, down. There was nothing else to do, so Alice soon began talking again. "Dinah'll miss me very much to-night, I should think!" (Dinah was the cat.) "I hope they'll remember her saucer of milk at tea-time. Dinah, my dear! I wish you were down here with me! There are no mice in the air, I'm afraid, but you might catch a bat, and that's very like a mouse, you know. But do cats eat bats, I wonder?" And here Alice began to get rather sleepy, and went on saying to herself, in a dreamy sort of way, "Do cats eat bats? Do cats eat bats?" and sometimes "Do bats eat cats?" for, you see, as she couldn't answer either question, it didn't much matter which way she put it. She felt that she was dozing off, and had just begun to dream that she was walking hand in hand with Dinah, and was saying to her, very earnestly, "Now, Dinah, tell me the truth: did you ever eat a bat?" when suddenly, thump! thump! down she came upon a heap of sticks and dry leaves, and the fall was over.

Alice was not a bit hurt, and she jumped up on to her feet in a moment: she looked up, but it was all dark overhead: before her was another long passage, and the White Rabbit was still in sight, hurrying down it. There was not a moment to be lost: away went Alice like the wind, and was just in time to hear it say, as it turned a corner, "Oh my ears and whiskers, how late it's getting!" She was close behind it when she turned the corner, but the Rabbit was no longer to be seen: she

found herself in a long, low hall, which was lit up by a row of lamps hanging from the roof.

There were doors all round the hall, but they were all locked; and when Alice had been all the way down one side and up the other, trying every door, she walked sadly down the middle, wondering how she was ever to get out again.

Suddenly she came upon a little three-legged table, all made of solid glass: there was nothing on it but a tiny golden key, and Alice's first idea was that this might belong to one of the doors of the hall; but, alas! either the locks were too large, or the key was too small, but at any rate it would not open any of them. However, on the second time round, she came upon a low curtain she had not noticed before, and behind it was a little door about fifteen inches high: she tried the little golden key in the lock, and to her great delight it fitted!

Alice opened the door and found that it led into a small passage, not much larger than a rat-hole: she knelt down and looked along the passage into the loveliest garden you ever saw. How she longed to get out of that dark hall, and wander about among those beds of bright flowers and those cool fountains, but she could not even get her head through the doorway; "and even if my head *would* go through," thought poor Alice, "it would be of very little use without my shoulders. Oh, how I wish I could shut up like a telescope! I think I could, if I only knew how to begin." For, you see, so many out-of-the-way things had happened lately, that Alice had begun to think that very few

things indeed were really impossible.

There seemed to be no use in waiting by the little door, so she went back to the table, half hoping she might find another key on it, or at any rate a book of rules for shutting people up like telescopes: this time she found a little bottle on it ("which certainly was not here before," said Alice), and tied around the neck of the bottle was a paper label, with the words "DRINK ME" beautifully printed on it in large letters.

It was all very well to say "Drink me," but the wise little Alice was not going to do *that* in a hurry. "No, I'll look first," she said, "and see whether it's marked '*poison*' or not"; for she had read several nice little stories about children who had got burnt, and eaten up by wild beasts, and other unpleasant things, all because they *would* not remember the simple rules their friends had taught them: such as, that a red-hot poker will burn you if you hold it too long; and that, if you cut your finger very deeply with a knife, it usually bleeds; and she had never forgotten that, if you drink much from a bottle marked "poison," it is almost certain to disagree with you, sooner or later.

However, this bottle was *not* marked "poison," so Alice ventured to taste it, and, finding it very nice (it had, in fact, a sort of mixed flavour of cherry-tart, custard,

pine-apple, roast turkey, toffy, and hot buttered toast), she very soon finished it off.

"What a curious feeling!" said Alice. "I must be shutting up like a telescope!"

And so it was indeed: she was now only ten inches high, and her face brightened up at the thought that she was now the right size for going through the little door into that lovely garden. First, however, she waited for a few minutes to see if she was going to shrink any further: she felt a little nervous about this; "for it might end, you know," said Alice to herself, "in my going out altogether, like a candle. I wonder what I should be like then?" And she tried to fancy what the flame of a candle looks like after the candle is blown out, for she could not remember ever having seen such a thing.

After a while, finding that nothing more happened, she decided on going into the garden at once; but, alas for poor Alice! when she got to the door, she found she had forgotten the little golden key, and when she went back to the table for it, she found she could not possibly reach it: she could see it quite plainly through the glass, and she tried her best to climb up one of the legs of the table, but it was too slippery; and when she had tired herself out with trying, the poor little thing sat down and cried.

"Come, there's no use in crying like that!" said Alice to herself rather sharply.

"I advise you to leave off this minute!" She generally gave herself very good advice (though she very seldom followed it), and sometimes she scolded herself so severely as to bring tears into her eyes; and once she remembered trying to box her own ears for having cheated herself in a game of croquet she was playing against herself, for this curious child was very fond of pretending to be two people. "But it's no use now," thought poor Alice, "to pretend to be two people! Why, there's hardly enough of me left to make *one* respectable person!"

Soon her eye fell on a little glass box that was lying under the table: she opened it, and found in it a very small cake, on which the words "EAT ME" were beautifully marked in currants. "Well, I'll eat it," said Alice, "and if it makes me grow larger, I can reach the key; and if it makes me grow smaller, I can creep under the door: so either way I'll get into the garden, and I don't care which happens!"

She ate a little bit, and said anxiously to herself "Which way? Which way?", holding her hand on the top of her head to feel which way it was growing; and she was quite surprised to find that she remained the same size. To be sure, this is what generally happens when one eats cake; but Alice had got so much into the way of expecting nothing but out-of-the-way things to happen, that it seemed quite dull and stupid for life to go on in the common way.

So she set to work, and very soon finished off the cake.

Halloween Blessing

by Sabrina Dearborn

At this time of dark and night,
spirits often give a fright.
We call upon the ancient dead,
circling now around our head.
Bring the blessings from before,
while we stand with open door.
Ancient spirits hear us now,
peace and love do we avow.

MIRRORS

Be careful never to break a mirror. It's a long seven years of bad luck that it will bring. Should a mirror fall and break on its own, a death in the home is soon expected. Even the house where the mirror is broken is thought to remain cursed for seven years. You also invite bad luck when you look at your reflection in a mirror by candlelight.

Long ago, people looked in amazement at their reflections in water, believing it was a glimpse at their soul. When the reflected image was altered by a wave or a ripple, it meant the soul was in danger. Over time, it came to be believed that if someone broke a mirror, it took seven years for their soul to return to them.

The seven-year sentence was assigned by the Romans, who believed it took a body seven years to repair itself or, in this case, seven years to shake the bad luck.

All Hallows' Eve

Halloween is a celebration of spooks and goblins, mysteries and magic. What is now called Halloween actually evolved from an ancient European holiday known as All Hollows' Eve: the day supernatural spirits were known to wander the earth. It began as the ancient Celtic festival of Samhain, which marked the moment when the veil between the living and the dead was lifted, and inhabitants of the two worlds could commune. For some 2000 years, October 31st meant bidding goodbye to summer, welcoming winter, and remembering the dead. Samhain marked the death of the old year and the birth of the next. It was a day of the dead, a night of magic and divination, a time when ghosts and lost souls roamed the land.

According to legend, every Samhain the souls of the dead were set free by the Lord of the Dead. It was believed that many of these spirits then roamed the natural world searching for bodies to possess. Families began dressing in scary disguises and noisily marching around their neighborhoods to scare away these immortal souls. This practice became the origin of the modern Halloween traditions of wearing costumes and committing harmless pranks.

So the next time you are choosing what to be for Halloween, remember all those spirits looking for a strong healthy body to inhabit, and pick a costume that is truly terrifying—it just might save your soul.

EYEBALL POTION

A must-have for any Halloween party! Blindfold your guests before asking them to put their hands into this bowl of goop! When they feel those slimy wet grapes between their fingers, they'll think they're touching eyeballs for sure!

1 lb. red or green grapes
4 cups water
1 large box of Cherry Jello Powder (8 servings size)

1. Peel the skin off of the grapes and set aside in a large Pyrex bowl.
2. In a medium size pot, over medium heat bring 2 cups water to a simmer. Add Jello and stir. Continue to simmer until consistency is completely smooth. Remove from heat, add 2 cups cold water, and pour over bowl of grapes. Stir well. Refrigerate for 3 hours or until Jello is firm.
3. Remove from refrigerator a few hours before the party and allow Jello mixture to sit at room temperature.

THE LEGEND OF SLEEPY HOLLOW

BY WASHINGTON IRVING

In the bosom of one of those spacious coves which indent the eastern shore of the Hudson, at that broad expansion of the river denominated by the ancient Dutch navigators the Tappan Zee, and where they always prudently shortened sail, and implored the protection of St. Nicholas when they crossed, there lies a small market town or rural port, which by some is called Greensburgh, but which is more generally and properly known by the name of Tarry Town. Not far from this village, perhaps about two miles, there is a little valley, or rather lap of land, among high hills, which is one of the quietest places in the whole world. A small brook glides through it, with just murmur enough to lull one to repose; and the occasional whistle of a quail, or tapping of a woodpecker, is almost the only sound that ever breaks in upon the uniform tranquility.

From the listless repose of the place, and the peculiar character of its inhabitants, who are descendants from the original Dutch settlers, this sequestered glen has long been known by the name of Sleepy

Hollow, and its rustic lads are called the Sleepy Hollow Boys throughout all the neighboring country. A drowsy, dreamy influence seems to hang over the land, and to pervade the very atmosphere. Some say that the place was bewitched by a high German doctor, during the early days of the settlement; others, that an old Indian chief, the prophet or wizard of his tribe, held his pow-wows there before the country was discovered by Master Hendrick Hudson. Certain it is, the place still continues under the sway of some bewitching power, that holds a spell over the minds of the good people, causing them to walk in a continual reverie. They are given to all kinds of marvellous beliefs; are subject to trances and visions; and frequently see strange sights, and hear music and voices in the air. The whole neighborhood abounds with local tales, haunted spots, and twilight superstitions; stars shoot and meteors glare oftener across the valley than in any other part of the country, and the nightmare, with her whole ninefold, seems to make it the favorite scene of her gambols.

The dominant spirit, however, that haunts this enchanted region, and seems to be commander-in-chief of all the powers of the air, is the apparition of a figure on horseback without a head. It is said by some to be the ghost of a Hessian trooper, whose head had been carried away by a cannon-ball, in some nameless battle during the Revolutionary War, and who is ever and anon seen by the country folk, hurrying along in the gloom of night, as if on the wings of the wind. His haunts are not confined to the valley, but extend at times to the

adjacent roads, and especially to the vicinity of a church at no great distance. Indeed, certain of the most authentic historians of those parts, who have been careful in collecting and collating the floating facts concerning this spectre, allege that the body of the trooper, having been buried in the churchyard, the ghost rides forth to the scene of battle in nightly quest of his head; and that the rushing speed with which he sometimes passes along the Hollow, like a midnight blast, is owing to his being belated, and in a hurry to get back to the churchyard before daybreak.

Such is the general purport of this legendary superstition, which has furnished materials for many a wild story in that region of shadows; and the spectre is known, at all the country firesides, by the name of the Headless Horseman of Sleepy Hollow.

In this by-place of nature, there abode, in a remote period of American history, that is to say, some thirty years since, a worthy wight of the name of Ichabod Crane; who sojourned, or, as he expressed it, "tarried," in Sleepy Hollow, for the purpose of instructing the children of the vicinity.

His school-house was a low building of one large room, rudely constructed of logs; the windows partly glazed, and partly patched with leaves of old copy-books. It was most ingeniously secured at vacant hours by a whithe twisted in the handle of the door, and stakes set against the window-shutters; so that, though a thief might get in with

perfect ease, he would find some embarrassment in getting out: an idea most probably borrowed by the architect, Yost Van Houten, from the mystery of an eel-pot. The school-house stood in a rather lonely but pleasant situation, just at the foot of a woody hill, with a brook running close by, and a formidable birch-tree growing at one end of it.

The schoolmaster is generally a man of some importance in the female circle of a rural neighborhood; being considered a kind of idle, gentleman-like personage, of vastly superior taste and accomplishments to the rough country swains, and, indeed, inferior in learning only to the parson. His appearance, therefore, is apt to occasion some little stir at the tea-table of a farm-house, and the addition of a supernumerary dish of cakes or sweet-meats, or, peradventure, the parade of a silver tea-pot. Our man of letters, therefore, was peculiarly happy in the smiles of all the country damsels. How he would figure among them in the churchyard, between services on Sundays! gathering grapes for them from the wild vines that overrun the surrounding trees; reciting for their amusement all the epitaphs on the tombstones; or sauntering, with a whole bevy of them, along the banks of the adjacent mill-pond; while the more bashful country bumpkins hung sheepishly back, envying his superior elegance and address.

Another of his sources of fearful pleasure was, to pass long winter evenings with the old Dutch wives, as they sat spinning by the fire, with a row of apples roasting and spluttering along the hearth, and lis-

ten to their marvellous tales of ghosts and goblins, and haunted fields, and haunted brooks, and haunted bridges, and haunted houses, and particularly of the headless horseman, or Galloping Hessian of the Hollow, as they sometimes called him. He would delight them equally by his anecdotes of witchcraft, and the direful omens and portentous sights and sounds in the air, which prevailed in the earlier times of Connecticut; and would frighten them woefully with speculations upon comets and shooting stars, and with the alarming fact that the world did absolutely turn round, and that they were half the time topsy-turvy!

Among the musical disciples who assembled, one evening in each week, to receive his instructions in psalmody, was Katrina Van Tassel, the daughter and only child of a substantial Dutch farmer. She was a blooming lass of fresh eighteen; plump as a partridge; ripe and melting and rosy-cheeked as one of her father's peaches, and universally famed, not merely for her beauty, but her vast expectations.

Ichabod Crane had a soft and foolish heart towards the sex; and it is not to be wondered at that so tempting a morsel soon found favor in his eyes; more especially after he had visited her in her paternal mansion. Old Baltus Van Tassel was a perfect picture of a thriving, contented, liberal-hearted farmer. He seldom, it is true, sent either his

eyes or his thoughts beyond the boundaries of his own farm; but within those everything was snug, happy, and well-conditioned. He was satisfied with his wealth, but not proud of it; and piqued himself upon the hearty abundance rather than the style in which he lived. His stronghold was situated on the banks of the Hudson, in one of those green, sheltered, fertile nooks in which the Dutch farmers are so fond of nestling. A great elm-tree spread its broad branches over it; at the foot of which bubbled up a spring of the softest and sweetest water, in a little well, formed of a barrel; and then stole sparkling away through the grass, to a neighboring brook, that bubbled along among alders and dwarf willows.

From the moment Ichabod laid his eyes upon these regions of delight, the peace of his mind was at an end, and his only study was how to gain the affections of the peerless daughter of Van Tassel. In this enterprise, however, he had more real difficulties than generally fell to the lot of a knight-errant of yore, who seldom had anything but giants, enchanters, fiery dragons, and such like easily conquered adversaries, to contend with; and had to make his way merely through gates of iron and brass, and walls of adamant, to the castle-keep, where the lady of his heart was confined; all which he achieved as easily as a man would carve his way to the centre of a

Christmas pie; and then the lady gave him her hand as a matter of course. Ichabod, on the contrary, had to win his way to the heart of a country coquette, beset with a labyrinth of whims and caprices, which were forever presenting new difficulties and impediments; and he had to encounter a host of fearful adversaries of real flesh and blood, the numerous rustic admirers, who beset every portal to her heart; keeping a watchful and angry eye upon each other, but ready to fly out in the common cause against any new competitor.

Among these the most formidable was a burly, roaring, roistering blade, of the name of Abraham, or, according to the Dutch abbreviation, Brom Van Brunt, the hero of the country round, which rang with his feats of strength and hardihood. He was broad shouldered and double-jointed, with short, curly black hair, and a bluff but not unpleasant countenance, having a mingled air of fun and arrogance. From his Herculean frame and great powers of limb, he had received the nickname of Brom Bones, by which he was universally known.

Brom, who had a degree of rough chivalry in his nature, would fain have carried matters to open warfare, and have settled their pretensions to the lady according to the mode of those most concise and simple reasoners, the knights-errant of yore—by single combat; but Ichabod was too conscious of the superior might of his adversary to enter the lists against him: he had overheard a boast of Bones, that he would "double the schoolmaster up, and lay him on a shelf of his own school-house;" and

he was too wary to give him an opportunity. There was something extremely provoking in this obstinately pacific system; it left Brom no alternative but to draw upon the funds of rustic waggery in his disposition, and to play off boorish practical jokes upon his rival. Ichabod became the object of whimsical persecution to Bones and his gang of rough riders. They harried his hitherto peaceful domains; smoked out his singing-school, by stopping up the chimney; broke into the schoolhouse at night, in spite of its formidable fastenings of withe and window-stakes, and turned everything topsy-turvy: so that the poor schoolmaster began to think all the witches in the country held their meetings there. But what was still more annoying, Brom took opportunities of turning him into ridicule in presence of his mistress, and had a scoundrel dog whom he taught to whine in the most ludicrous manner, and introduced as a rival of Ichabod's to instruct her in psalmody.

In this way matters went on for some time, without producing any material effect on the relative situation of the contending powers. On a fine autumnal afternoon, Ichabod, in pensive mood, sat enthroned on the lofty stool whence he usually watched all the concerns of his little literary realm. In his hand he swayed a ferule, that sceptre of despotic power; the birch of justice reposed on three nails, behind the throne, a constant terror to evil-doers; while on the desk before him might be seen sundry contraband articles and prohibited weapons, detected upon the persons of idle urchins; such as half-munched apples, pop-guns, whirligigs, fly-cages, and whole legions of rampant little

paper game-cocks. Apparently there had been some appalling act of justice recently inflicted, for his scholars were all busily intent upon their books, or slyly whispering behind them with one eye kept upon the master; and a kind of buzzing stillness reigned throughout the school-room. It was suddenly interrupted by the appearance of a negro, in tow-cloth jacket and trousers, a round-crowned fragment of a hat, like the cap of Mercury, and mounted on the back of a ragged, wild, half-broken colt, which he managed with a rope by way of halter. He came clattering up to the school-door with an invitation to Ichabod to attend a merry-making or "quilting frolic," to be held that evening at Mynheer Van Tassel's; and having delivered his message with that air of importance, and effort at fine language, which a negro is apt to display on petty embassies of the kind, he dashed over the brook, and was seen scampering away up the Hollow, full of the importance and hurry of his mission.

All was now bustle and hubbub in the late quiet school-room. The scholars were hurried through their lessons, without stopping at trifles; those who were nimble skipped over half with impunity, and those who were tardy had a smart application now and then in the rear, to quicken their speed, or help them over a tall word. Books were flung aside without being put away on the shelves, inkstands were overturned, benches thrown down, and the whole school was turned loose an hour before the usual time, bursting

forth like a legion of young imps, yelping and racketing about the green, in joy at their early emancipation.

The gallant Ichabod now spent at least an extra half-hour at his toilet, brushing and furbishing up his best and indeed only suit of rusty black, and arranging his locks by a bit of broken looking-glass, that hung up in the school-house. That he might make his appearance before his mistress in the true style of a cavalier, he borrowed a horse from the farmer with whom he was domiciliated, a choleric old Dutchman, of the name of Hans Van Ripper, and, thus gallantly mounted, issued forth, like a knight-errant in quest of adventures. But it is meet I should, in the true spirit of romantic story, give some account of the looks and equipments of my hero and his steed. The animal he bestrode was a broken-down plough-horse, that had outlived almost everything but his viciousness. He was gaunt and shagged, with a ewe neck and a head like a hammer; his rusty mane and tail were tangled and knotted with burrs; one eye had lost its pupil, and was glaring and spectra; but the other had the gleam of a genuine devil in it. Still he must have had fire and mettle in his day, if we may judge from the name he bore of Gunpowder.

Ichabod was a suitable figure for such a steed. He rode with short stirrups, which brought his knees nearly up to the pommel of the saddle; his sharp elbows stuck out like grasshoppers'; he carried his whip perpendicularly in his hand, like a sceptre, and, as his horse jogged on, the motion of his arms was not unlike the flapping of a pair of wings.

It was toward evening that Ichabod arrived at the castle of the Heer Van Tassel, which he found thronged with the pride and flower of the adjacent country. Old farmers, a spare leathern-faced race, in homespun coats and breeches, blue stockings, huge shoes, and magnificent pewter buckles. Their brisk withered little dames, in close crimped caps, long-waisted shortgowns, homespun petticoats, with scissors and pincushions, and gay calico pockets hanging on the outside. Buxom lasses, almost as antiquated as their mothers, excepting where a straw hat, a fine ribbon, or perhaps a white frock, gave symptoms of city innovation. The sons, in short square skirted coats with rows of stupendous brass buttons, and their hair generally queued in the fashion of the times, especially if they could procure an eel-skin for the purpose, it being esteemed, throughout the country, as a potent nourisher and strengthener of the hair.

Brom Bones, however, was the hero of the scene, having come to the gathering on his favorite steed, Daredevil, a creature, like himself, full of mettle and mischief, and which no one but himself could manage. He was, in fact, noted for preferring vicious animals, given to all kinds of tricks, which kept the rider in constant risk of his neck, for he held a tractable well-broken horse as unworthy of a lad of spirit.

Old Baltus Van Tassel moved about among his

guests with a face dilated with content and good-humor, round and jolly as the harvest-moon. His hospitable attentions were brief, but expressive, being confined to a shake of the hand, a slap on the shoulder, a loud laugh, and a pressing invitation to "fall to, and help themselves."

And now the sound of the music from the common room, or hall, summoned to the dance. The musician was an old gray-headed negro, who had been the itinerant orchestra of the neighborhood for more than half a century. His instrument was as old and battered as himself. The greater part of the time he scraped on two or three strings, accompanying every movement of the bow with a motion of the head; bowing almost to the ground, and stamping with his foot whenever a fresh couple were to start.

When the dance was at an end, Ichabod was attracted to a knot of the sager folks, who, with old Van Tassel, sat smoking at one end of the piazza, gossiping over former times, and drawing out long stories about the war.

But all these were nothing to the tales of ghosts and apparitions that succeeded. The neighborhood is rich in legendary treasures of the kind. Local tales and superstitions thrive best in these sheltered long-settled retreats; but are trampled underfoot by the shifting throng that forms the population of most of our country places. Besides, there is no encouragement for ghosts in most of our villages, for they have

scarcely had time to finish their first nap, and turn themselves in their graves before their surviving friends have travelled away from the neighborhood; so that when they turn out at night to walk their rounds, they have no acquaintance left to call upon. This is perhaps the reason why we so seldom hear of ghosts, except in our long-established Dutch communities.

The immediate cause, however, of the prevalence of supernatural stories in these parts was doubtless owing to the vicinity of Sleepy Hollow. There was a contagion in the very air that blew from the haunted region; it breathed forth an atmosphere of dreams and fancies infecting all the land. Several of the Sleepy Hollow people were present at Van Tassel's and, as usual, were doling out their wild and wonderful legends. Many dismal tales were told about funeral trains, and mourning cries and wailings heard and seen about the great tree where the unfortunate Major André was taken, and which stood in the neighborhood. Some mention was made also of the woman in white, that haunted the dark glen at Raven Rock, and was often heard to shriek on winter nights before a storm, having perished there in the snow. The chief part of the stories, however, turned upon the favorite spectre of Sleep Hollow, the headless horseman, who had been heard several times of late, patrolling the country; and, it was said, tethered his horse nightly among the graves in the churchyard.

All these tales, told in that drowsy undertone with which men talk in the dark, the countenances of the listeners only now and then

receiving a casual gleam from the glare of a pipe, sank deep in the mind of Ichabod. He repaid them in kind with large extracts from his invaluable author, Cotton Mather, and added many marvellous events that had taken place in his native State of Connecticut, and fearful sights which he had seen in his nightly walks about the Sleepy Hollow.

The revel now gradually broke up. The old farmers gathered together their families in their wagons, and were heard for some time rattling along the hollow roads, and over the distant hills. Some of the damsels mounted on pillions behind their favorite swains, and their light-hearted laughter, mingling with the clatter of hoofs, echoed along the silent woodlands, sounding fainter and fainter until they gradually died away—and the late scene of noise and frolic was all silent and deserted. Ichabod only lingered behind, according to the custom of country lovers, to have a tête-à-tête with the heiress, fully convinced that he was now on the high road to success. What passed at this interview I will not pretend to say, for in fact I do not know. Something, however, I fear me, must have gone wrong, for he certainly sallied forth, after no very great interval, with an air quite desolate and chop-fallen.—Oh, these women! these women! Could that girl have been playing off any of her coquettish tricks?—Was her encouragement of the poor pedagogue all a mere sham to secure her

conquest of his rival?—Heaven only knows, not I!—Let it suffice to say, Ichabod stole forth with the air of one who had been sacking a hen-roost, rather than a fair lady's heart. Without looking to the right or left to notice the scene of rural wealth on which he had so often gloated, he went straight to the stable, and with several hearty cuffs and kicks, roused his steed most uncourteously from the comfortable quarters in which he was soundly sleeping, dreaming of mountains of corn and oats, and whole valleys of timothy and clover.

It was the very witching time of night that Ichabod, heavy-hearted and crestfallen, pursued his travel homewards, along the sides of the lofty hills which rise above Tarry Town, and which he had traversed so cheerily in the afternoon. The hour was as dismal as himself. Far below him, the Tappan Zee spread its dusky and indistinct waste of waters, with here and there the tall mast of a sloop riding quietly at anchor under the land. In the dead hush of midnight he could even hear the barking of the watch-dog from the opposite shore of the Hudson; but it was so vague and faint as only to give an idea of his distance from this faithful companion of man. Now and then, too, the long-drawn crowing of a cock, accidentally awakened, would sound far, far off, from some farm-house away among the hills—but it was like a dreaming sound in his car. No signs of life occurred near him, but occasionally the melancholy chirp of a cricket, or perhaps the gutteral twang of a bull-frog, from a neighboring marsh, as if sleeping uncomfortably, and turning suddenly in his bed.

All the stories of ghosts and goblins that he had heard in the afternoon, now came crowding upon his recollection. The night grew darker and darker; the stars seemed to sink deeper in the sky, and driving clouds occasionally hid them from his sight. He had never felt so lonely and dismal. He was, moreover, approaching the very place where many of the scenes of the ghost-stories had been laid. In the centre of the road stood an enormous tulip-tree, which towered like a giant above all the other trees of the neighborhood, and formed a kind of landmark. Its limbs were gnarled, and fantastic, large enough to form trunks for ordinary trees, twisting down almost to the earth, and rising again into the air. It was connected with the tragical story of the unfortunate André, who had been taken prisoner hard by; and was universally known by the name of Major André's tree. The common people regarded it with a mixture of respect and superstition, partly out of sympathy for the fate of its ill-starred namesake, and partly from the tales of strange sights and doleful lamentations told concerning it.

As Ichabod approached this fearful tree, he began to whistle: he thought his whistle was answered,—it was but a blast sweeping sharply through the dry branches. As he approached a little nearer, he thought he saw something white, hanging in the midst of the tree,—he paused and ceased whistling; but on looking more narrowly, perceived that it was a place where the tree had been scathed by lightning, and the white wood laid bare. Suddenly he heard a groan,—his teeth chattered and his knees smote against the saddle: it was but the rubbing of one huge bough upon another, as they were swayed about by the breeze. He passed the tree in safety; but new perils lay before him.

About two hundred yards from the tree a small brook crossed the road, and ran into a marshy and thickly wooded glen, known by the name of Wiley's swamp. A few rough logs, laid side by side, served for a bridge over this stream. On that side of the road where the book entered the wood, a group of oaks and chestnuts, matted thick with wild grape-vines, threw a cavernous gloom over it. To pass this bridge was the severest trial. It was at this identical spot that the unfortunate André was captured, and under the covert of those chestnuts and vines were the sturdy yeomen concealed who surprised him. This has ever since been considered a haunted stream, and fearful are the feelings of the school boy who has to pass it alone after dark.

As he approached the stream, his heart began to thump; he summoned up, however, all his resolution, gave his horse half a score of kicks in the ribs, and attempted to dash briskly across the bridge; but instead of starting forward, the perverse old animal made a lateral movement, and ran broadside against the fence. Ichabod, whose fears increased with the delay, jerked the reins on the other side, and kicked lustily with the contrary foot: it was all in vain; his steed started, it is true, but it was only to plunge to the opposite side of the road into a thicket of brambles and alder bushes. The schoolmaster now bestowed both whip and heel upon the starveling ribs of old Gunpowder, who dashed forward, snuffling and snorting, but came to a stand just by the bridge, with a suddenness that had nearly sent his rider sprawling over his head. Just at this moment a plashy tramp by the side of the bridge caught the sensitive ear of Ichabod. In the dark shadow of the grove, on the margin of the brook, he beheld something huge, misshapen, black, and towering. It stirred not, but seemed gathered up in the gloom, like some gigantic monster ready to spring upon the traveller.

The hair of the affrighted pedagogue rose upon his head with terror. What was to be done? To turn and fly was now too late; and besides, what chance was there of escaping ghost or goblin, if such it was, which could ride upon the wings of the wind? Summoning up, therefore, a show of courage, he demanded in stammering accents—"Who are you?" He received no reply. He repeated his demand in a still more agitated voice. Still there was no answer. Once more he cudgelled the sides of the inflexible Gunpowder, and, shutting his eyes, broke forth with involuntary fervor into a psalm-tune. Just then the shadowy object of alarm put itself in motion, and, with a scramble and a bound, stood at once in the middle of the road. Though the night was dark and dismal, yet the form of the unknown might now in some

degree be ascertained. He appeared to be a horseman of large dimensions, and mounted on a black horse of powerful frame. He made no offer of molestation or sociability, but kept aloof on one side of the road, jogging along on the blind side of old Gunpowder, who had now got over his fright and waywardness.

Ichabod, who had no relish for this strange midnight companion, now quickened his steed, in hopes of leaving him behind. The stranger, however, quickened his horse to an equal pace. Ichabod pulled up, and fell into a walk, thinking to lag behind,—the other did the same. His heart began to sink within him; he endeavored to resume his psalm-tune, but his parched tongue clove to the roof of his mouth, and he could not utter a stave. There was something in the moody and dogged silence of this pertinacious companion, that was mysterious and appalling. It was soon fearfully accounted for. On mounting a rising ground, which brought the figure of his fellow-traveller in relief against the sky, gigantic in height, and muffled in a cloak, Ichabod was horror-struck, on perceiving that he was headless!—but his horror was still more increased, on observing that the head, which should have rested on his shoulders, was carried before him on the pommel of the saddle: his terror rose to desperation; he rained a shower of kicks and blows upon Gunpowder, hoping, by a sudden movement, to give his companion the slip,—but the spectre started full jump with him. Away then they dashed, through thick and thin; stones flying, and sparks flashing at every bound. Ichabod's flimsy garments fluttered in the air,

as he stretched his long lank body away over his horse's head, in the eagerness of his flight.

They had now reached the road which turns off to Sleepy Hollow; but Gunpowder, who seemed possessed with a demon, instead of keeping up it, made an opposite turn, and plunged headlong downhill to the left. This road leads through a sandy hollow, shaded by trees for about a quarter of a mile, where it crosses the bridge famous in goblin story, and just beyond swells the green knoll on which stands the white-washed church.

As yet the panic of the steed had given his unskillful rider an apparent advantage in the chase; but just as he had got half-way through the hollow, the girths of the saddle gave way, and he felt it slipping from under him. He seized it by the pommel, and endeavored to hold it firm, but in vain; and had just time to save himself by clasping old Gunpowder round the neck, when the saddle fell to the earth, and he heard it trampled underfoot by his pursuer. For a moment, the terror of Hans Van Ripper's wrath passed across his mind—for it was his Sunday saddle; but this was no time for petty fears; the goblin was hard on his haunches; and (unskillful rider that he was!) he had much ado to maintain his seat; sometimes slipping on one side, sometimes on another, and sometimes jolted on the high ridge of his horse's backbone, with a violence that he verily feared would cleave him asunder.

An opening in the trees now cheered him with the hopes that the church-bridge was at hand. The wavering reflection of a silver star

in the bosom of the brook told him that he was not mistaken. He saw the wall of the church dimly glaring under the trees beyond. "If I can but reach that bridge," thought Ichabod, "I am safe." Just then he heard the black steed panting and blowing close behind him; he even fancied that he felt his hot breath. Another convulsive kick in the ribs, and old Gunpowder sprang upon the bridge; he thundered over the resounding planks; he gained the opposite side; and now Ichabod cast a look behind to see if his pursuer should vanish, according to rule, in a flash of fire and brimstone. Just then he saw the goblin rising in his stirrups, and in the very act of hurling his head at him. Ichabod endeavored to dodge the horrible missile, but too late. It encountered his cranium with a tremendous crash,—he was tumbled headlong into the dust, and Gunpowder, the black steed, and the goblin rider, passed by like a whirlwind.

The next morning the old horse was found without his saddle, and with the bridle under his feet, soberly cropping the grass at his master's gate. Ichabod did not make his appearance at breakfast;—dinner-hour came, but no Ichabod. The boys assembled at the school-house, and strolled idly about the banks of the brook; but no schoolmaster. Hans Van Ripper now began to feel some uneasiness about the fate of poor Ichabod, and his saddle. An inquiry was set on foot, and after diligent investigation they came upon his traces. In one part of the

road leading to the church was found the saddle trampled in the dirt; the tracks of horses' hoofs deeply dented in the road, and evidently at furious speed, were traced to the bridge, beyond which, on the bank of a broad part of the brook, where the water ran deep and black, was found the hat of the unfortunate Ichabod, and close beside it a shattered pumpkin.

The brook was searched, but the body of the schoolmaster was not to be discovered.

The mysterious event caused much speculation at the church on the following Sunday. Knots of gazers and gossips were collected in the churchyard, at the bridge, and at the spot where the hat and pumpkin had been found. The stories of Brouwer, of Bones, and a whole budget of others, were called to mind; and when they had diligently considered them all, and compared them with the symptoms of the present case, they shook their heads, and came to the conclusion that Ichabod had been carried off by the Galloping Hessian. As he was a bachelor, and in nobody's debt, nobody troubled his head any more about him. The school was removed to a different quarter of the Hollow, and another pedagogue reigned in his stead.

It is true, an old farmer, who had been down to New York on a visit several years after, and from whom this account of the ghastly adventure was

received, brought home the intelligence that Ichabod Crane was still alive; that he had left the neighborhood, partly through fear of the goblin and Hans Van Ripper, and partly in mortification at having been suddenly dismissed by the heiress; that he had changed his quarters to a distant part of the country; had kept school and studied law at the same time, had been admitted to the bar, turned politician, electioneered, written for the newspapers, and finally had been made a justice of the Ten Pound Court. Brom Bones too, who shortly after his rival's disappearance conducted the blooming Katrina in triumph to the altar, was observed to look exceedingly knowing whenever the story of Ichabod was related, and always burst into a hearty laugh at the mention of the pumpkin; which led some to suspect that he knew more about the matter than he chose to tell.

The old country wives, however, who are the best judges of these matters, maintain to this day that Ichabod was spirited away by supernatural means; and it is a favorite story often told about the neighborhood round the winter evening fire. The bridge became more than ever an object of superstitious awe, and that may be the reason why the road has been altered of late years, so as to approach the church by the border of the millpond. The school-house, being deserted, soon fell to decay, and was reported to be haunted by the ghost of the unfortunate pedagogue; and the plough-boy, loitering homeward of a still summer evening, has often fancied his voice at a distance, chanting a melancholy psalm-tune, among the tranquil solitudes of Sleepy Hollow.

WIZARD'S GLASS TRICK

This dinner-table trick will show your family and friends you're a magic wizard with amazing powers of balance.

Hold up a bread plate and glass, showing your audience that there are no strings, glue or other props at work. Grasp the plate as shown in the illustration, with your thumb pointing upward.

With the back of the plate always hidden from the audience, place a glass on the top rim of the plate and support it with your thumb. Swerve the plate slightly to give the impression that you're using all your superhuman skills to keep the glass balanced.

Invite others at the table to try the trick—and be ready to catch the glass (if it's breakable) before it falls. When everyone begs you to show them how it's done, demand a price—like extra dessert.

Revenge an Enemy Spell

This spell is not to be taken lightly and should only be used when all other non-magical remedies have failed. If you wish to stop the antics or trickery of an enemy and get revenge, this time-honored charm will work without fail. Simply write the name of your

rival on a small piece of paper, roll it into a tiny ball, and place it in an empty mug along with a strand of the person's hair. Fill the mug with water and, as you hide it away in the depths of your freezer, recite aloud, "May your teeth chatter and your stomach grow fatter!" The moment the water hardens into ice, the spell will take effect. But be warned! If the ice should melt, the spell will be instantly broken. So defrost at your own risk!

acknowledgements

'The Foundling" from THE FOUNDLING AND OTHER TALES OF PRYDAIN by Lloyd Alexander. Copyright, © 1973 by LLoyd Alexander. Reprinted by permission of Henry Holt and Company, LLC.

"The Troll" by Ray Bradbury. Reprinted by permission of Don Congdon Associates, Inc. Copyright © 1991 by Ray Bradbury.

"Halloween Blessing" © by Sabrina Dearborn. From A CHILD'S BOOK OF BLESSINGS by Barefoot Books.

"Transylvania Dreaming" from MAKING FRIENDS WITH FRANKENSTEIN Copyright © 1994 Colin McNaughton. Reproduced by permission of the publisher Candlewick Press Inc., Cambridge, MA, on behalf of Walker Books Ltd., London

"Midnight Express" by Alfred Noyes. The Society of Authors as the Literary Representative of the Estate of Alfred Noyes.

"Harry" by Rosemary Timperley. Reproduced by permission of The Agency (London) Ltd. © Rosemary Timperley Credit to be given to first publication. All rights reserved and enquires to The Agency (London) Ltd. 24 Pottery Lane, London W11 4LZ fax: 0171 727 9037

Excerpt from THE HOBBIT. Copyright © 1966 by J.R.R. Tolkein. Reprinted by permission of Houghton Mifflin Co. All rights reserved.

ILLUSTRATIONS
pg. 34, 61: Arthur Rackham; pg.82-83, 162-163, 276, 310-311: John Winsch; pg.93: Harold C. Earnshaw; pg. 151: E.C. Banks; pg. 178-179: K. Lederbogen; pg. 182: Harrison Cody; pg. 188-189: Seherin; pg. 193: Edmund Dulac; pg. 198-199, 269: Hilda Austin; pg. 203: Alfons Mucha; pg. 233: Ellen H. Claysaddle; pg. 253: R. Drang; pg. 258: Jessie Willcox Smith; pg. 337: Bufforo

RECIPES © 2001 by Lena Tabori
ADDITIONAL ORIGINAL TEXT by Antonia Felix, Katrina Fried, Kathleen King, Chris Meason
Magic trick illustrations by Megan Halsey

Every attempt has been made to obtain permission to reproduce materials protected by copyright. Where omissions may have occurred, the publisher will be happy to acknowledge this in future printings.